Hellfire & Damnation

Hellfire & Damnation

by Connie Corcoran Wilson

The Merry Blacksmith Press

2011

Hellfire & Damnation

© 2011 Connie Corcoran Wilson

Introduction © 2011 William F. Nolan

For information, address:

The Merry Blacksmith Press
70 Lenox Ave.
West Warwick, RI 02893

merryblacksmith.com

Published in the USA by The Merry Blacksmith Press

ISBN— 978-0-61543-962-4

Table of Contents

Introduction
by William F. Nolan
(Logan's Run, Nightworlds)

LET ME START RIGHT OFF BY SAYING that Connie Wilson presents what I call "matter-of-fact" horror." She writes solid, declarative sentences rife with dark undertones. No fancy description for Connie. No sentimental musings. No soft emotionalism. Just hard-edged documentary-style storytelling. Jolting objective sentences made all the more disturbing by their cool directness. Frankly—and I consider myself well-read in the shock genre—I have never encountered a style such as she displays here, in story after story. Connie Wilson's dark talent is unique, and readers will stagger away from her icy tales, stunned and groggy.

Her "frame" for this collection is also unique: stories built around Dante's nine circles of hell. A unifying concept that is classically fresh.

Many of these hellish tales are based on truth, amplified into fiction. Her four stories set along Route 66 from Missouri through California are all true ghost stories. The final statements of convicted prisoners on Death Row, as they await execution, provide their actual words in "Hotter than Hell."

Connie's settings and backgrounds are beautifully variant: ancient Pompeii with zombie prostitutes, the Hmong people during the Vietnamese Secret War in Laos, the Amish community in Iowa. And the author explores her own hometown area of Moline, Illinois, in the brutally shocking "An American Girl," which is factually based on the gruesome murder of a luckless teenager.

Once you've read this remarkably fresh collection, you'll emerge with some twisted new thoughts about clowns, bats, birds, serial killers, zombies, sadistic dentists and headless chickens.   And what about the good folks in "Confessions of an Apotemnophile," who yearn to have their legs amputated?

Believe me, Dear Reader, you've never encountered anything like *Hellfire & Damnation.*

I have a final word for it…*WOW!*

From the Author

THE FOLLOWING COLLECTION of stories is connected thematically by Dante's *Inferno*. You, Gentle Reader, will enter through the **Gates of Hell.** You will travel through stories representing Dante's nine circles of hell:

> **Circle One**, Limbo
> **Circle Two**, Lust
> **Circle Three,** Gluttony
> **Circle Four,** Hoarders and Wasters
> **Circle Five,** the Wrathful
> **Circle Six,** Heresy
> **Circle Seven**, the Violent
> **Circle Eight,** the Fraudulent and
> **Circle Nine,** the Treacherous

The story that begins the collection and takes us through the Gates of Hell, *Hotter than Hell,* was inspired by listening to the Georgia Prison Tapes online, which feature the Death Row last words of condemned prisoners. All details in the story are true and actually happened during real executions; the continuous clanging noise of the prison gates in the background is haunting. The thoughts are those of actual Death Row inmates.

The fate of condemned prisoner Number 155371, Big Jim Bingham, of the Georgia Diagnostic and Classification State Prison in Jackson, will start us on our journey through **The Gates of Hell**.

Read further, if you dare, gentle reader, but: *"Abandon hope, all ye who enter here."*

Hotter Than Hell

INMATE #155371: James "Big Jim" Bingham, Death Row, Cell Block Number Nine, Georgia Diagnostic and Classification Prison in Jackson, Georgia (just off I-75 South, heading towards Macon). The first envelope reached Georgia on October 15, 1990. Badly damaged en route from Kuwait, the letter was hand-delivered to Big Jim Bingham by Darryl Presley, the warden.

Usually, the warden didn't bother with mail. It wasn't on his list of daily duties. But this letter had come all the way from Kuwait. Warden Presley had heard them talking about it in the mailroom. And, of course, there was the fact that Big Jim Bingham had only four months to live. He'd be executed in Butts County, Georgia, on February 22, 1991, joining twenty-nine others who had gone before, including both his sons, Jed and Lyle Bingham. And the world would be a better place, as far as Warden Darryl Presley was concerned.

"Who-in-the-hell do ya' think is writin' Big Jim, fellas?" he said to the guards on Death Row, as he half-walked, half-ambled John Wayne style, towards Big Jim's cellblock. "We got ourselves one hundred and twelve men on Death Row. Some of 'em have visitors. But have any of you known Big Jim to have a visitor since that second wife of his died of cancer? What was her name…Maizie?"

"No, Sir, Warden Presley, Sir! Big Jim don't get no visitors of any kind. Never has." Bob Mulligan wiped his nose with a dirty handkerchief that normally dangled from his pocket as he agreed with the warden. It was always smart to agree with Warden Presley. The warden had a mean streak.

The warden examined the envelope again. He looked at it as though he could read the contents of the sealed envelope with X-ray vision if he stared at it long and hard enough.

He rounded the corner, arriving at James Bingham's small cell.

"Hey, Jim! You got yourself a letter here! You got mail, boy!"

Bingham looked up from the Bible he was reading and gave the warden a cool stare.

"Didn't know you had any relatives left, Jim. That last wife of yours… Maizie…didn't she up and die on you a few years back? And we both know what happened to Lyle and Jed."

Warden Presley actually smiled at Jim when he said that.

"So, who's writin' you from Kuwait? You got yourself a new mail-order girlfriend? I'm just curious…just wonderin'." Warden Presley grinned at his clever comment.

Bingham didn't say anything. He just glared at the warden with ice-cold eyes. Eyes like a fish or a snake. Jim was tempted to make one of the Elvis jokes that the men in the yard liked to make about the warden's last name. Instead, he took the letter, put it in his Bible, and went on reading. James Bingham would be executed on February 22, 1991, God willing, and the river don't rise. He wasn't in much of a talking mood, and he sure wasn't going to read this letter while the warden watched him do it.

The mention of Jim's sons, Lyle and Jed, had pretty much riled him up inside. Big Jim had talked Lyle and Jed into helping him with the contract killing of Stanley Felker's wife, Fanny. Jim knew Stanley Felker from work at the IBP Beef Processing plant just outside town. Stanley Felker wasn't happy that Fanny Felker was screwing his best friend.

Jim and Lyle and Jed went to the Felkers' house and found Fanny and her boyfriend fucking on the living room couch. Fanny Felker fucking. Jim smiled at the alliteration. It was the last time Fanny fucked anyone. But the plan sure got fucked-up fast.

Things started to go wrong almost immediately. The boyfriend, his pants down around his ankles, escaped, bloody and wounded. Jim threw Fanny to the floor, put his gun next to her left ear, and pulled the trigger, even though, right up until he pulled back the hammer, she was screamin' and cryin' fit to kill.

Just before Jim shot her, she shrilled, "Please don't kill me! I'll do anything! Don't kill me!" Fanny's nose was running. She was a mess and stank of KY jelly and cheap lavender perfume.

"You're gonna' die, bitch," Jim said. He was a man of few words and fewer moral scruples. Fanny was a tart. Jim didn't mind killing useless things. Fanny's whoring around ended with Jim's bullet to her temple. Jim didn't think any more about killing Fanny than he did that time he drowned the kittens the boys wanted to keep.

Jed and Lyle, aged five and seven, pleaded, "Please don't do it, Daddy! Don't kill 'em!" But Big Jim had killed 'em, anyway. They was just kittens, after all. And Fanny was just a cheatin' wife. No big deal. It was just too bad they got caught. It was too damned bad that Lyle and Jed had such piss-poor legal representation or they might not have got the chair. At least Jim's lawyer had managed to keep him alive till now. But Lyle and Jed? They was gone.

Lyle and Jed Bingham were executed six months apart. One guard told Jim that Lyle had "danced with the devil in the pale moonlight," as though Lyle's jerking in the electric chair was humorous. But Lyle's death went smoothly, compared to Jed's. They really botched the job with Jed. In fact, the story of Jed Bingham's botched execution caused the state of Georgia to change to lethal injection as its preferred killing method.

There were three men throwing three switches at Jed's execution. When they sent the first surge of electricity through Jed Bingham's 195-pound body, his body snapped forward like a Jack-in-the-box. Stage One, they called it. They shocked Jim's oldest boy Jed with seventeen hundred volts for five seconds. Then, the sons-of-bitches moved to Stage Two. Despite the revolting smell of burning flesh and the frenzied bobbing of Jed's hooded head and his wrists working frantically against the restraints of Old Sparky, fists balled, the good ol' boys gave him another one thousand volts for seven seconds. Stage Three: two hundred and eight volts for another seven seconds, just for good measure.

There was always a six-minute cool-down period before the doctors could go into the chamber and check the convict's vital signs and pronounce him dead. But Jed wasn't dead.

At 12:22 a.m. Bob Mulligan, presiding officer, said, "He's still breathin'. From where I am, I can see his head bobbin' up and down. I think he's still breathin', Commissioner! What should we do?"

Bob was semi-frenzied. He was sweating like a boxer in the middle of a bout. He looked frazzled and fried, himself. The smell was getting to all the witnesses, and the dull, echoing background noise of heavy prison doors slamming elsewhere in the building didn't do much for anyone's mood. One female reporter looked like she was going to vomit; the guy from the local TV station did. Then it really stank in the close quarters of the chamber, even though the guards hustled the TV anchorman with the queasy stomach outside, pronto. Six inches of fire flashed from the electrode on Jed's left leg. Blood soaked his shirt, coming from underneath the hood.

At 12:26 a.m. Jed Bingham received 2,908 volts of electricity in three waves, but he was still fighting for life; he might give out, but he wouldn't give up. He took twenty-three breaths. At 12:28 a.m. he snapped upright in the chair. His fists balled again. There was still a terrible stench of burning flesh; in the distance, the clanging of doors continuing, over and over, throughout the execution. It was as though the gates of hell were clanging open and shut.

"What should we do, Commissioner?" Mulligan looked worried and upset as he clutched the phone, talking to the Warden's office where Commissioner Crandall had come down from the capitol for the spectacle.

"Check him and go through it again." That was the merciless verdict of Commissioner Crandall. Safely away from the scene in Warden Presley's office, he was havin' himself a nice fat stogie and a glass of Scotch.

"Right. We gonna' do it again," responded Mulligan. Later, the cons in the yard would have a good laugh over "doing a Mulligan," like in golf.

Do it again; they did. Jed struggled. Six inches of electrical fire flamed from the top of his head. His charred head bobbed and then sank to his chest. Jed…his oldest boy and the second of his sons to be executed for taking part in the contract killing of Fanny Felker…was finally dead. God…or the devil…rest his soul.

Back in Big Jim's cell, Warden Presley had handed Jim his letter and left. Or, as the inmates liked to say behind Presley's back, sniggering, "Elvis has left the building."

Big Jim Bingham, now alone in his cell, opened his first letter in over five years in prison. It was from his third and only surviving son, Frank.

Frank and his mother Molly had left for Chicago right after Big Jim's second arrest for drugs. Molly divorced Jim as soon as she hit Illinois, and that was that. Jim never heard from either of them again, until now.

"Dear Dad," the letter began, in cramped printed-in-pencil block letters.

"You don't really know me. When Mom took me to Chicago to live, you were still back in Georgia. I was just a baby. Two years old. I've been told that Lyle and Jed was, like, twenty and twenty-two. I don't really remember you, either.

Now, I'm twenty-two. I'm here in Kuwait, waiting to cross the border and move into Iraq to stop Saddam Hussein from taking over Kuwait. It isn't right for a country that is just sitting there, minding its own business, to be invaded by a bigger, more powerful country. I agree with President Bush that we gotta' stop him. He's a bad man. Bad for his country and bad for the world. Those kinds of people should be stopped from doing evil, especially against innocent people who can't defend themselves.

So, I'm here in Kuwait, and it's hotter than hell! Word is that we will move out in the next ninety days to cross the border and do some real fighting. I sure hope so, 'cause all this sittin' around doing nothing stinks. We have drills for poison gas, and the stupid masks and suits are so Goddamned hot that you almost up and die from that alone. This place is hell on Earth. It is real bad here in every way. But I know that I'm a soldier doing the right thing, for once, and I'm a soldier for God in my mind, too, because I did some bad things, myself, when I was younger. When she was mad at me, Mom would always yell at me, 'The apple don't fall far from the tree.' I think she meant you. That's why I joined the Army after I graduated high school. I coulda' gone to college, but I wanted to serve my country and help stop bad men from doing evil in the world, and I needed to make up for some bad stuff of my own, too, before it's too late.

I know that your execution date is February 22nd. I hope that I can get a pass to come be with you, but I don't know if I can, yet. I'll write more when I know.

If you want to write me, here is my address."

It was signed, "Your son, Frank."

Jim read the letter three times, top to bottom. Then, he took out a small piece of paper:

"Dear Frank,

It was good to hear from you. I don't get no mail. I don't have no visitors, either.

You sound like you turned out real good in life. I think that's because your mother had some people with money back there in Chicago. I know she went to live with her sister, at first, and she got herself a college degree. She was always real smart. Too smart for me.

My time is running out on Earth; it's just caving in on me. I realize that. My execution will show what society really thinks of poor people. We've been used, and we'll continue to be used. Those that have money are the ones that get by. If you have money to hire yourself a good lawyer, you get off. It's as simple as that. I wish Jed had had a better lawyer. What they did to that boy was a cryin' shame. Nobody should die like he did. Those devils should all rot in hell for what they did to Jed, and for what they did to Lyle, too. And for what they want to do to me.

I am not sorry that I got Jed and Lyle involved in killing Fanny Felker, 'cause Fanny Felker needed killin', but I'm sorry we got caught.

I hope you can come, when they put me down. I feel like this line from that Mother Goose poem, 'Katy Cruel:' 'That I was where I would be, then I should be where I am not. Here I am, where I must be. Where I would be, I cannot.' Just like you.

I send you all my love. Do not be bitter. Work hard in the Army. Stay safe.

Thanks for writing me.

Your father,

Jim Bingham."

The second letter, dated November 15, 1990, came a month later. This time, it wasn't hand-delivered by the warden. It repeated that the food, the K-rations, were bad, the country desolate. "A shit-hole," young Frank called it.

The third letter arrived in December, 1990. Frank described the local people and how they had been hateful towards the troops. "Even the little kids want to kill us. I hate these fuckers," he wrote. He didn't sound as committed to the cause as he had at the beginning of his tour of duty, nor as idealistic. This letter also said that the authorities would not let Frank return to the United States for the execution; only for Jim's funeral, they said.

The letter dated January 15, 1991, was on the pillow of Jim's cot when he returned from the forty-five minutes he got in the exercise yard, alone, hot and sweaty from lifting weights and running. It was shorter than the first two. It, too, talked about the conditions, the heat, the barrenness. It talked about how there was nothing at all to do; that it seemed like an eternity since he had seen his mom.

The next letter came a week later on January 22, 1991, exactly one month before Jim's execution date. It, too, was on Big Jim's bed when the guards led him back to his cell in shackles.

"Hi, Dad!

"I'll bet you've been wondering what I've been up to. Well, not much. It's pretty boring here, and I haven't been doing much of anything.

I really wonder what we are put on Earth for? I thought I was going to help stop a bad guy, but I wonder, now, since I think we were only sent here to get oil for the USA. Man! I hate dying for some Fat Cat greedy bastard's big ol' bank account. But it seems like that's just the way it is for poor people. The ones with the power don't care about us, except to use us to get what they want.

Well, I don't want to bring you down. I know you'll only have a few weeks to go when you get this. As you know from my earlier letter, I can't come be with you. They won't let me. I'll write again.

Your son,

Frank"

The final letter arrived a month later, the day of Frank's execution. Jim had been busy with Prison Chaplain Wardell Boggs. He was being prepped and making last statements and ordering his last meal. He hadn't been this busy since he ran drugs in Jackson and shot Fanny Felker.

Just as he was about to open the letter from Frank that had materialized on his cot like the last two, an Army representative in full uniform shouldered his way into the cell. He was holding a small cardboard box, and he had an uncomfortable expression on his green-tinged face.

"I'm sorry, James. These were your son's personal effects. He wanted you to have them. He was killed in combat on January 15, 1991, by a sniper, just after his unit crossed over the border from Kuwait to Iraq."

Jim was speechless. He looked at the dates on his letters: October 15, 1990; November 15, 1990; December 12, 1990; January 15, 1991. The January 22, 1991, letter had no postmark. Today's letter also had no postmark of any kind. It was dated February 20, 1991. How was this possible? There must be some mistake. It must be the time that it took for letters to get back to the states from overseas… Jim *died* January 15, 1991! *No! Please, God. Anything but that!* Jim's world came crashing in on him again.

Jim sank to his bunk, asked to be left alone, and covered his face with his hands. He examined the contents of the box: a copy of Joseph Conrad's "Heart of Darkness"; a Bible; a tattered copy of Dante's "Inferno"; some girlie magazines; a deck of cards, a pair of sunglasses. When he finally recovered enough to do so, he ripped open the final, crumpled, scribbled, pencil-written letter, the one dated February 20th, more than a month after his son lay dead.

"Hi, Dad!

I wanted to write and say it's not too bad here. It's boring and repetitive. Like life. If your execution is carried out, know that it will be God's will; we get what we deserve. Or do we? Maybe it's the way things work in the US of A? We get what poor people in the United States always get: screwed. Or is this what happens to bad guys like us?

People look at convicts and soldiers as being between humans and animals. Just look at how many homeless nut-case vets are out there, roamin' the streets, beggin' for money for food or booze. Remember how our nation welcomed home the Vietnam vets? Ha! Convicts ain't treated no better, either. No real attempt to understand or help. Just remember: we Binghams might give out, but we don't give up.

I know you been readin' the good book. I hope you are a new creature now, like I am, instead of the cold-blooded psycho killer that got Jed and Lyle killed for shooting Fanny Felker.

I want you to know: I'll be waitin' for you. I've been waitin' for you for a while now. Jed and Lyle are waitin' here, too.

And I was wrong, Dad, when I said Kuwait was hotter than hell. I was wrong.

Your son,
Frank."

Circle One: Limbo

LIMBO IS DESCRIBED AS A PLACE that is neither heaven nor hell. Pagan souls were said to end up in limbo, if they were not Christians at the time of their death. In Catholic theology, the souls of infants or other young children who died in original sin but free of grievous personal sin ended up in Limbo indefinitely.

The term "limbo" has become part of the language, meaning an undetermined state or period of time. Even if the Catholic Church decrees that Limbo no longer exists, it exists for Rachel and David of this story.

Rachel and David

This strange ghost story has been circulating in Webster Groves, Missouri for many years...

WHEN MIKE AND I MOVED INTO THE OLD HOUSE at 334 North Gore Street between North Rock Hill Road and West Kirkham Avenue in Webster Groves, Missouri, we were intrigued by the handsome stone structure, the Rock House, our next-door neighbor.

"Wow! Look at that!" Mike's awe at the beauty of this National Historic Landmark was evident in his voice. It was a great-looking place. The building had housed the Edgewood Children's Center for emotionally disturbed children next door to our new rental since 1944.

"It's gorgeous, isn't it?" I said, as we carried boxes from our U-Haul to the shabby-chic old house we had just rented as our new home. The landlord had seemed very glad to rent the place to us. We found out why when we settled in and discovered the extent of the renovation that was going to be necessary to make the house livable. Faulty plumbing. Creaking floorboards. Old furnace. The full complement of trouble.

"It's a good thing our rent's so low, or I'd consider moving to a fancier neighborhood." Mike was smiling. He hugged me hard, too, and patted my pregnant stomach. I knew he was just having fun at my expense. We both loved the large leafy oak trees of Webster Groves and the grand houses that stood all around us. Our house might be a bit more run-down than the rest, but we were moving up in the world, for sure.

"Awwww! Don't be like that. This is a terrific neighborhood. Why, the trees around here have to be at least one hundred and fifty years old! I read somewhere that a lot of this area was built around the time of the

World's Fair in St. Louis. Don't you think this street looks just like that Judy Garland movie?"

"What Judy Garland movie?"

"You know…the one where she sang 'Clang! Clang! Clang went the trolley!'" I sang the verse, to get Mike's full attention, just as he was plugging in a standing lamp, only to discover that the electricity to the outlet seemed to be non-functioning.

"Oh! That's 'Meet Me in St. Louis.'"

"Louie?" I asked, with a laugh. Mike came over and hugged me tight once again.

"You better not be meeting anybody named Louie. You're my wife, and I'm very happy that you are." He kissed me softly on the cheek and returned to the lamp.

"Just think, Meg. It's our very own home. Our first house."

"Rented house," I reminded him with a grin, just to keep things real.

We were newlyweds, married just shy of a year. Up until now, we had been living in cramped apartment quarters. One place we lived, we even had to go down the hall to use the community bathroom, so "our very own place," as Mike had dubbed the run-down two-story frame house seemed palatial to us. We were ready, willing and able to start a family. This would be a great house for a child. I was four months pregnant, but I wasn't showing, yet. Mike had just been appointed regional manager of the new chain shoe store down the road at the mall. Life was looking up.

The chill in the late October air made the fireplace inviting, but a small disaster with the flue left us banging on the ancient radiators. We prayed the heat would kick in before we turned to Popsicles. We were having trouble making anything work in the decrepit old house.

"Let's huddle together for warmth," Mike said, laughing.

"You just want an excuse to huddle. I'm not sure it's for warmth." I hugged him in return. "And we both know where that impulse has gotten us." Just then, our attention was caught by a redheaded boy of about twelve, approaching our house from the direction of next door's Children's Center.

"Straighten up and fly right, Boy-Oh. Wouldn't do to terrorize the neighbors. Especially since they're all supposed to be children with emotional issues already." The doorbell rang.

A ruddy-faced carrot-topped boy of about twelve stood there on the porch when I opened the door, clipboard and pen in his hand. Behind him, clutching a toy stuffed unicorn and silently regarding us with big blue eyes was a little girl who looked about six years old, presumably his younger sister.

"Hello, Mrs." He said, in a courtly old-fashioned manner. "Would you care to order a Christmas wreath from the Edgewood Children's Center? It's not much money. We'll deliver the wreath to you a month before Christmas. We're just taking orders now."

He looked so eager to please and was so polite that Mike and I both said, in unison, "How much?"

"Only ten dollars. They're real. Blue spruce. It'll smell great, and it'll look great on the front door of this fine house." He smiled. Apparently the redheaded entrepreneur was not above a little insincere flattery. Anything to make a sale.

"What's your name?" we asked simultaneously.

"David." He shuffled from foot to foot, the cold wind making his ruddy cheeks appear rosier.

"You cold, David?" I asked.

"Yes, Ma'am."

"Want to come just inside the door while I give you our information? And maybe you'd like a cookie? We have some Oreos in the kitchen somewhere." Mike and I were addicted to Oreos, always arguing about eating them "the proper way." We had made sure before we packed the kitchen stuff in our former apartment that the Oreos would be right on top, so that we could have a quick pick-me-up of sugar whenever we wished. And, of course, we could also have our favorite debate over the "proper way" to eat an Oreo, with me favoring the white filling first and the cookie last, and Mike the reverse. We joked that we were like Jack Spratt and his Mrs. from the famous nursery rhyme.

"I'd like a cookie, Ma'am, but what's an Oreo?" asked the shy, polite boy, as he stepped inside.

"You've never heard of Oreo cookies?"

"Oh! So it's a type of cookie, then?"

"Why, yes. Yes, it is." I didn't know anyone who wouldn't recognize the brand name.

"What about your little sister?" I asked David. The girl was lingering on the sidewalk. She had not climbed even one step up towards the top of the porch stoop.

"Oh, Rachel won't come in. She don't talk."

"Can she have an Oreo?" I asked. In this day and age, you had to be careful about handing out candy or cookies to strange children.

"Sure, but she won't say please and thank you, proper-like. It's just her way. She don't talk. And she won't come inside, either. She got scared real bad. After that, she just quit talking." I wanted to ask what had scared the poor thing that badly, but I didn't want to pry into personal matters.

"That's okay. If she can stand the cold, we'll give her an Oreo to eat outside while she waits for you. It won't take but a minute to give you our information. Her pet unicorn can have one, too." As I said this, I extended two Oreo cookies towards the silent girl with the gigantic blue limpid pools for eyes, who was staring at me and clutching the pink stuffed unicorn as though it could save her.

Rachel took the first cookie and held it to the stuffed unicorn's pink mouth. The unicorn did not take a bite. No surprise there. Rachel held the second cookie in her hand, her fingers clutched tightly around it. She made no move to put the Oreo in her mouth. Silence.

"Well, Rachel, we'll have your brother back in a flash. Feed that unicorn while you wait." I smiled in what I hoped was a kindly fashion as I shut the door against the cold. I could see that Rachel had not moved even one foot from the spot on the sidewalk she had chosen. She grasped the Oreos firmly in her slender fingers, uneaten.

"Our address is 334 North Gore Street, David, but we don't have our phone hooked up, yet. We're the Hansens…Mike and Meg Hansen."

"Oh, that's okay, Mrs. Hansen. We'll deliver the wreaths personal-like, but not till one month before Christmas. I'll collect the ten dollars then."

"That sounds fine, David. And don't forget your cookie!" David turned to leave as I almost forgot to give the young salesman his reward. I remarked, "It wouldn't do to give your sister, Rachel, TWO cookies and not give you even one!"

"It's okay, Mrs. Hansen. Rachel won't mind. She knows I'd do anything for her. She'd share her cookies with me, if you forgot." And then he was gone, giving us a last sad lingering look over his shoulder. He walked down the three steps to the sidewalk and rejoined his waiting sister and her pet unicorn. He took Rachel by the hand. They walked toward the cottonwood tree in the backyard of the Edgewood Children's Center, fading into the haze of swirling smoke from autumn bonfires in the neighborhood of large trees.

Pyrite benzene, I thought to myself as the children disappeared in the haze from the burning leaves. *Nasty stuff. That stuff can kill you. Those kids shouldn't play near that bonfire. The people who work at the center should keep them away from that smoke. I hope the children don't have asthma.*

In the two weeks that followed, we learned more about the history of the Edgewood Children's Center, researching it on the Internet. The children's home was over one hundred and seventy-five years old. Originally, the St. Louis Association of Ladies had established it for "the relief of orphan children" after the cholera epidemic of 1832. In 1834, the ladies came to the aid of the poor orphans, founding the Center. By 1848, the place had been renamed the Saint Louis Protestant Orphans' Asylum. The asylum wasn't located next door to us on Gore Street then, though. It had only moved to the Rock House, as it was known, in 1869. The Reverend Artemus Bullard, a preacher, operated a seminary for young men in the Rock House next door until he was tragically killed in a train wreck in 1855.

Reverend Bullard was a strong believer in the abolition of slavery. The Rock House was one of the stops on the Underground Railroad. A tunnel several blocks long ran beneath the Rock House. Slaves from the South routinely hid there on their way North to freedom. In 1890, two children became lost in the tunnel and died. After that, the exit was sealed off.

In 1910 a fire gutted the old Rock House. The interior was destroyed, but the lovely stone exterior remained just as we saw it daily through our kitchen window. A six-year-old girl perished in the blaze that year, although her older brother tried to rescue her and died in the conflagration himself.

As we continued to unpack our few belongings, following David and Rachel's departure, a middle-aged lady wearing a plaid Burberry muffler picked up our package of paper plates. Dislodged from the kitchen goods, the package of plates had taken flight in the strong gusty winds of the late October afternoon chill. The plates behaved almost like a giant pack of Frisbees.

"Here you go," the stranger said with a laugh, as she placed the plain Chinette plate package she had retrieved from the street into my chilly hands.

"Thanks so much," I said. "I was afraid I was going to have to break out my track shoes to catch those things. And who knows where *they* are?" I laughed and extended my hand. "That wind is really fierce. Thanks from Meg and Mike Hansen, your new neighbors." I hoped my smile conveyed my genuine gratitude at the friendly gesture from the white-clad stranger, the first adult we had met in our new neighborhood.

"Not a bit," she said, shaking my hand. "I'm Lucinda Resnick. I was just getting off my shift at the center. I stay through the nights on Mondays, Wednesdays and Fridays. But, since it's Thursday, I get to go home and actually cook and care for my own family."

"You have children at home?" I asked. My question came more from curiosity than politeness. I wondered how the woman could manage to stay overnight next door while supervising active children of her own at home.

"Oh, yes. My husband is a fireman. He works weird shifts that we can usually coordinate. You know...week on, week off stuff. I really love kids, including my own," she said, smiling. "These kids need me more even than my own, though, because most of them have emotional problems. Different traumas, you know. It didn't start out that way, of course. The home originally was for orphans from the 1832 cholera epidemic, but, over the years, and with the move here to Rock House, today's kids all seem to have psychological problems. You know the drill. Kid comes home and finds his father hanging in the basement. Parents leave to play golf and Mom and Dad never come home, killed in a car accident. Eventually, many of those kids wind up here." She said all this so matter-of-factly that I was impressed with her efficient, calm demeanor.

"Well, it's wonderful work that you do," I said. And I meant it. "We met the young redheaded boy, David, and his sister, Rachel, just an hour or so ago. They seemed like such nice, polite young people. Although it's sad that Rachel doesn't speak. Why is that? Do you know?" I had been wondering about the small, frail six-year-old with the big blue eyes and the pink stuffed unicorn pet, clutching her Oreo cookies and waiting patiently for her older brother. Wondering why Rachel didn't speak. What unspeakable horror had her young blue eyes seen?

Lucinda seemed startled. "David? When did you meet David?"

I turned to Mike for confirmation. "It was an hour ago, right?" I asked Mike. He was hammering away at a loose step on the front porch, two nails in his mouth, and nodded assent.

"Yes, an hour ago David came selling Christmas wreaths. Reasonably priced ones, too. We ordered one and gave him a cookie. His sister, Rachel, wouldn't come inside, although we gave her an Oreo, too. David said she doesn't speak. He was such a courtly young gentleman. Very Old World. So polite and courteous." I smiled at Lucinda, expecting her to smile in response. Instead, she wore a puzzled expression, so I went on, "I don't think I've ever met a child or an adult who didn't know what an Oreo was, though. I had to explain to David that an Oreo is a cookie."

"How old was this David?" Lucinda asked.

"About twelve. Why?"

"We have a David at the center…the only one," Lucinda explained, "but our David is six feet two with dark hair. David Leibovitz. He's Jewish. He wouldn't be selling Christmas wreaths."

"What about Rachel?" I asked. "Do you have a Rachel? Little girl of six? Big blue eyes?"

"Yes and no," Lucinda finally said, with great reluctance.

"What do you mean? You *do* have a Rachel? A small six-year-old who won't speak? Or you *don't* have a small girl with big blue eyes who just stares at you as though she's clairvoyant or something?" I had noticed the unusual nature of Rachel's gaze. I felt uneasy as she stared at me, while her friendlier older brother chatted to us about the wreath.

"There was a young girl named Rachel in the home many years ago. She had an older brother named David. Both were orphaned by the flu epidemic, and so they came to live at Edgewood. Near Christmas in 1910, the house caught fire. Rachel was trapped in an upstairs bedroom. David died trying to rescue her. Sometimes, people say they can still see a red glow in the upstairs bedroom on the right. That was Rachel's room. There are residents who claim to have seen Rachel swinging in the swing hung up in the old cottonwood tree. Others say she floats in the air near there, especially at Halloween. Of course, you can't believe what kids say when it's Halloween, now, can you?"

"Did Rachel have a pink stuffed animal…a unicorn?"

"How did you know?" Lucinda asked. She opened her car door, preparatory to leaving.

"I saw them both…remember?"

Lucinda quickly slammed the door to her car shut without further comment. She started the car and drove away, no longer our friendly new neighbor, but a spooked white-clad nurse from the institution next door who probably thought we were both nuts.

Mike finished nailing the loose porch boards. We both just stood there, absorbing everything we had just heard. Neither of us felt threatened; we both just felt infinitely sad.

"Do you remember that neither one of them ate the Oreos?" I asked. "In fact, David didn't even know what an Oreo was!"

"Well, to be fair, the unicorn didn't eat the Oreo, either," Mike said.

"The unicorn is a mythical beast, Mike." I sounded cross. I was really just struggling to understand the unknowable. I was spooked.

"My point, exactly," said Mike, as he opened the door to our home at 334 North Gore Street, and we returned to reality. "Guess we should just plan on picking up a wreath ourselves when we get our Christmas tree," he added, with a crooked smile.

"Funny. Very funny."

I moved to the computer and quickly googled Oreo cookies. 1912. Oreo cookies weren't invented until 1912. The fire that killed both children occurred in 1910.

We hugged each other and moved to the couch in front of the fireplace, as a chill pervaded the room.

"Mike?" I asked.

"Yeah." He settled deeper into the comfy chintz couch and pulled me towards him.

"When we have the baby, if it's a boy, let's name it David."

Mike looked at me seriously. His eyes crinkled with understanding. "And if it's a girl?"

"Rachel, of course."

The fire crackled in the fireplace, warming the cold room, and I almost could swear that I smelled the crisp aroma of blue spruce.

Circle Two: Lust

THIS STRANGE TALE OF A YOUNG GIRL sold into prostitution is also a tribute to the enduring nature of true love.

But lust is not just the province of the young, as we learn in the true story of the ghost of the Skirvin Hotel, known simply as Effie…

Love Never Dies

I WAS LED INTO THE BROTHEL IN POMPEII by Sittius Nucerino Veterano on the tenth of August. We entered from one of the two nearby secondary roads. As we entered the brothel courtyard, we passed a statue of Priapus standing near a fig tree. Priapus was holding one of two huge phalluses in his hand. He was so large that a string-like apparatus was suspended from the second of his giant penises, to help suspend the organ in the air. My eyes grew wide with astonishment and curiosity. *Is this what a naked man looks like?* I thought.

I was only twelve years old. I had never seen a naked adult male body, let alone a man who looked like this. I was a trophy of war, along with nine other undead chained virgins who followed me into the brothel. Sittius Nucerino Veterano had fought bravely for Caesar in the civil wars in Apice. He was now my owner.

"Sittius," said Caesar after the battle was won, "I wish to reward your courage and valor in battle. I have arranged for you to have the youngest and most beautiful prostitutes in Pompeii. There will be a never-ending supply of young virgins to work in your brothel. This endless bounty will be accomplished through the special offices of the necromancer, Claudius Rufus. Go to him at the Temple of Venus. He knows many secrets. With these secrets he will constantly repopulate your brothel with beautiful virgins. But there is a condition: the prostitutes are all recently deceased girls. They are females who died young. Their undead condition will make them more malleable as well as more passionate in bed. However," and here Caesar sniffed delicately, "there is one condition. They will be able to work as prostitutes for only three weeks. If you keep them longer, the stench of death will be unable to be disguised. After three weeks, each girl must be delivered to the crematorium for final disposal. This is my unique gift to you, in gratitude for your faithful service to me. You are to speak of it to no one." With that, the Master of the Known World walked off into the shadows near his tent.

"I thank you, my Lord," cried the famous warrior Sittius to Caesar's retreating back. Sittius was not sure he had been heard, but, as the son of another famous warrior, Sitto Nucerino Veterano, he knew he had just been greatly honored. Now would begin his new post-war life as brothel-keeper in Pompeii.

When Sittius visited the Temple of Venus, Claudius Rufus shared some of his many secrets. He repeated Caesar's explanation more fully. How was Sittius' brothel able to have so many virgins servicing its ten beds?

"Female children often die young in Pompeii, Sittius. But the Book of Necromancy stored here in the Temple of Venus has allowed me to bring these females back from the dead, to rejuvenate them. They are only able to return to mortal life temporarily, and then only as undead creatures. Their life must end permanently after three weeks. When three weeks passes, each zombie female must be taken to the House of Cryptoporticus, where a hidden crematorium will end their suffering and their wretched lives for the second and final time. Remember: the girls must not remain undead for more than twenty-one days. Not only would the stink offend your customers, but your very soul will be at risk if you fail to follow this edict of the gods, laid out in the Book of Necromancy. To defy this order would offend Proserpina, Goddess of the Underworld. I assume that I can trust you to do as I command?"

Sittius looked startled at learning so much information about so many forbidden topics. "Of course, your Excellency," he managed to gasp in reply. Although surprised, he asked Claudius Rufus an important question for an entrepreneur about to embark on a new career as a brothel keeper.

"But, Claudius Rufus…these young girls…Won't the stench of death offend the customers, anyway? Won't the men know?"

"For three weeks, no. The cosmetics such as black kohl that Egyptian women favor, Marc Antony's gift to Roman women, and the smell of lavender and other rich aromas will mask the smell of death and decay for three brief weeks. The women themselves will function as little more than slaves. The men's appetites will be satisfied. The undead make wonderful prostitutes. They are quiet, obedient and passive, true, but they provide a perfect receptacle for the living. Just remember: after three weeks you *must* deliver each dead girl to the House of Cryptoporticus for burning, or risk the consequences."

"What are the consequences?" asked Sittius.

"You don't want to know what the consequences are, noble Sittius. Content yourself with the huge profit you will receive in coin of the realm. Remember to honor the vow you have made to deliver each undead maiden to the House of Cryptoporticus when twenty-one suns have come and gone. And do not anger fair Proserpina, the Goddess of the Underworld." Claudius Rufus turned and exited.

"Yes, honorable Claudius Rufus. I will do exactly as you ask."

And so it came to pass that I walked through one of the two ground floor entrances of the brothel now owned by Sittius Nucerino Veterano, chained to the other girls. It was just two days after my parents had buried me in a quiet, cold tomb overlooking the sea, the victim of a mysterious fever. I was still clad in my white funeral gown; my fair hair was plaited with silver leaves, my face painted lightly with white powder. This white powder would soon give way to the heavier make-up of a Pompeii prostitute. Such make-up was necessary to cover the eventual decay and decomposition of my features.

I knew nothing of men.

I knew nothing of life.

I knew nothing of death, although I had experienced it once.

I was twelve years old. I had never lain with a man. All that was about to change.

As I walked past the table where an uneaten plate of pasta and beans remained, Sittius pointed to the wooden stairway and bade me climb it.

"There, girl. Go."

"My name is Livia."

"Then go, Livia. Climb to your quarters." He said this sternly, but not unkindly. I obeyed.

On the ground floor were two entrances and five beds, each with a bed built into the wall and a wooden door. I passed these beds before I began to climb to my own bed on the second floor. A short mattress covered the tops of the beds. The footsteps of visitors could be seen on the mattresses, marks left by the many men who had passed this way before. Most of the customers who left footprints were probably selecting the sex act they most wished to experience, picking it from among those pictured on the wall murals. The walls of the room contained scenes of various erotic games that the clients could request: anal sex, tantric sex, sex as the beasts in the field practice it, giant phalluses being suckled by fair maidens, male dominant sex, male-on-male sex, couples performing fellatio on one another, masochistic sex with bondage and pain, cunnilingus. All a customer need do was point out his particular desire. These pornographic details barely registered on me, a twelve-year-old virgin.

Fresh from the grave, I was approaching another kind of death. And I had overheard Sittius say to a nearby attendant that I was to be burned in twenty-one days. My fear was so great that I could barely breathe. Palms, clammy as the grave, fumbled at my embroidered white toga. I tried not to make eye contact with anyone, afraid of what would happen if I did. I imagined how horrible it would be to be alive and feel flames searing my feet. Burned alive! I had died once. I did not wish to die twice.

When I reached the top of the brothel, the second floor was more spacious. There was a projecting gallery with windows. My bed was near a window that overlooked a flower garden. More murals of erotic acts; five more beds greeted my not-yet-teen-aged eyes.

My new master, Sittius, indicated the bed nearest the window.

"This will be your station. See that you stay near it and service customers willingly. You will be fed twice a day. Watch and see what the other handmaidens do to their faces to make them attractive. Make sure that you use copious amounts of oil of lavender and other fragrances to mask the stench." Sittius, a short swarthy man with excessive hair on his chest and arms, ordered this and departed. I was released from the bondage of my chains and the other girls to whom I had been tethered were led away.

Another very young girl stationed beside the next bed hissed at me. She had long dark hair, in contrast to my fair blonde locks. She looked older than me and showed some visible signs of decaying flesh behind one ear if you looked closely, beneath her hairline.

"Psssst. What is your name? I'm Julia."

"My name is Livia."

"How old are you?"

"I'll be thirteen in a fortnight."

At this, Julia laughed. "I'm fourteen. I'm not a virgin. What do *you* know about pleasuring men?"

"Nothing," I said quietly. It was true. Julia began applying make-up, and I watched her closely and mimicked her actions.

"Will it hurt?" I asked. I was terrified at the very thought of sex with anyone.

"Yes…the first time," Julia responded. My knees grew weak. My fear of death and dying, and now fear of the sex act combined to make me stagger slightly. "Did you hear the men talk about burning us?" I asked.

"Burning? What?"

"Yes. I heard Sittius say that, after twenty-one days, we must be taken somewhere to be burned."

At this news, Julia grew deathly white. Her dark brown eyes widened in disbelief. She rushed to my side and whispered in my ear, "Come with me."

Julia led me to a remote corner of the loft that was slightly hidden from the others. "Tell me everything you know. And, before you do, remove your clothing."

"What? Why?" I had only my burial garment, and it was the finest gown I had ever owned. I repeated what I had heard about the crematorium.

"I want to show you something to help you prepare for the men who will come soon. Trust me. I won't hurt you. And this will help you."

I looked into her dark brown eyes, and I knew that I could trust her. I removed my white toga.

"Lie down on this cot," Jullia said.

I did as she asked.

"Spread your legs. It is necessary."

I was hesitant, but there was no turning back now. My nakedness and my fear made me shiver. I spread my legs wide and was surprised to see only the top of Julia's head, her lush brown hair shining in the dim light, the curls touching my inner thighs. Her hair felt as soft as cornsilk. I felt a butterfly lightness touch me inside. It was not unpleasant, and Julia had promised not to hurt me, so I said nothing. At first. As she continued, I could not keep from making a small sound. A sound of pleasure. A moan. In only moments, it felt as though some secret switch inside me had been turned on, a switch to pleasure that was hot like a bolt of lightning. I cried aloud.

Just then, Sittius' steps could be heard coming back upstairs and Julia hissed, "Quick! Put your robe back on!" I did so, and we stealthily returned to our stations, my legs wet from the juice of her lips and my own sexual readiness. Sittius took a look around at all the girls and left again. Julia and I resumed our talk.

"Julia…is that what it will feel like with the men?"

"No, Livia. The men care not if they hurt us or if we feel pleasure or pain. We are nothing but chattel to them. Only another woman, like me, can make you feel this way. I will help you. I will help you to be ready for your first time."

"But you are just a girl…like me."

"Yes, I am just a girl, but I know of life. I will help you find your way. Stay with me, and I will try to keep you safe. I have been here for fourteen days. I know how it will play out."

"But…Julia…if you have been here for fourteen days, you are in danger. The men will not let any of us linger past twenty-one days." A look passed across Julia's beautiful features like a cloud across the sky.

"Yes, " she said. "I have a plan. Tonight, after the visit of Mauritius the Gladiator, we will speak again."

When night came, so did the customers, coming from two secondary roads, the Via Stabiana and Via Degu Augustali.

Late in the evening Martius Titienses, a gladiator-in-training, arrived at the brothel. He was a major celebrity in Pompeii. Sweaty from his day's exertions practicing for gladiatorial combat against Christians, lions and other gladiators, practicing in order to please the Emperor, it was as though the Emperor himself had arrived. Everyone took notice. All the other girls, save Julia and me, were occupied with customers. All the other girls were also undead, zombies like us. But none was as young and beautiful… or as inexperienced… as me. And none were as fresh. Some who had been in the brothel for nearly three weeks were displaying signs of decomposition as they neared the twenty-one day deadline that would signal their second death. They were becoming rank. I, however, was fresh meat. Sittius wished to pay special homage to the famous gladiator Martius Titienses. He offered me, his freshest, youngest and most beautiful virgin, as the sexual partner of the famous man.

"Martius Titienses! It is an honor to have you in my house. Come… let me show you the newest of our girls. A virgin, she just arrived today." Sittius beckoned towards the stairwell, urging Martius to follow his lead.

"What is that smell?" asked Martius, following Sittius upstairs to the chamber.

"Smell? Oh! That! Why…see the uneaten beans and pasta? It is just the poor housekeeping of my maid. I will see that she clears it away quickly. She will be punished for her dereliction to duty. The young nymph who awaits you smells as fragrant as the flowers of the field."

That much was true. I had been anointed with lavender, lilac, various oils of flowers; I had lain in a cold tomb for only twelve hours before the stone was rolled back and the grave robbers snatched me. But now I also smelled faintly of sex, thanks to Julia's ministrations.

As Martius approached, I lowered my eyes to the floor. I did not know what to do. I was in awe of his fame. I felt unworthy of his attention, still wondering at my sudden transition from living child to corpse to undead maiden.

Martius addressed me directly. "Girl…what is your name?"

"Livia, Sir," I said, curtsying.

"Are you wise in the ways of the world? In the ways of men?"

I did not know how to answer this question. I responded as best I could with just a look. The smell of sweat from the tired gladiator, flowers from outside the window swirled in a rich stew of odors. I could smell my own fear and my own sexual juices and this aroma lingered in my nostrils. The mucous aroused by Livia's tongue, slowly dripped down my inner thigh as I awaited Martius' advances. The odor was not new to me… slightly fishy, slightly decadent…but now I wondered if the aroma meant sex or death. I was shaking.

"I do not know the ways of the world, good sir, but all in the city have heard of the famous Martius Titienses. I will do all in my power to please you." I summoned enough courage to raise my eyes to his; his eyes were kind, deep blue, bemused.

"Do you wish to spend some time with me?" His eyes twinkled as he asked.

"Yes, good sir. It would be an honor." I kept my eyes downcast. I did not want him to see my fear. I did not want him to sense my inexperience.

Martius Titienses removed the armored breastplate he had been wearing during his practice sessions that day. The copper-plated shield made a loud clank as it dropped to the floor. He put a small dagger under my pillow, a precaution against any unexpected attack from the outside world. Then, he stripped before me until he was as naked as the statue that had so startled me as I entered the brothel. Rather than two huge phalluses of epic proportions, Martius looked healthy, normal. I wished that I, too, were healthy and normal. I was neither, but Martius did not know this.

When he took me in his arms and began kissing me on the cheeks, lips and breasts, I felt something I had only felt once before, under Julia's ministrations. Even though I was dead, I felt alive. The color rose in my already-rosy cheeks. He gently touched me there thrusting two fingers deep inside me.

"You are wet, girl! You are ready!" As Martius said this, he smiled an encouraging smile and put just the tip of his rock-hard penis into my vagina. I was frightened, but I was excited. I felt a huge surge of emotion for Martius, yet I also remembered the gentle butterfly-like kisses of Julia with pleasure. Martius' penis was as erect and hard as that of the marble statue outside my window. I cried out only once, as he entered me. My hope was that he had not heard. The spreading stain on the mattress beneath me gave me away. Julia's kiss had not bloodied me, but now my white garment was stained. I grimaced in pain.

After we had finished making love, Martius touched my hair gently and laid me down on the bed, saying, "Sleep, Little One." I heard him speak with Sittius. I heard the clink of coins.

"No other man is to touch her. I will be back tomorrow. And purchase her a new garment with this money."

No other man was to touch me, but Martius had not said that Julia could not touch me. Julia and I lay together almost every day. I learned to love the smell of her hair, the touch of her skin. She would kiss me gently, arousing me just before the arrival of Martius, which occurred every evening at the same time.

Each night for three days Martius returned to the brothel. Each night, we made passionate love. Each time, thanks to Julia, I was ready for him. I waited for the sound of his voice, the touch of his hand and lips. When he was there or when I lay with Julia and she caressed me, I felt alive. At other times, I remained as dead as if still in the tomb.

After three days of torrid lovemaking with Martius, Julia approached me. She had now been resident in the brothel for seventeen days. In just four days, she would be taken to the crematorium, if what I had heard was true.

"Livia," she said. "You must help me. I don't want to die. I have already died once. In just four days I will be burned, unless you can help me."

"Julia, you know I care for you. You and Martius are the only friends I have in the world. I love you both dearly. How can I help you.?"

Julia sketched a bold plan whereby Martius, who seemed fond of me, would be asked to take me to the Temple of Venus, so that I could be made whole again. Because he seemed to care for me so much, Julia wanted me to enlist his help in securing our freedom. I promised to do whatever I could, but I was torn. Did I love Julia or did I love Martius? Did I love them both? How could I choose between them, when I loved each?

Julia had just four days to live, unless I secured Martius' help.

I knew that I must tell Martius the truth in order to gain his help. He could save me, if anyone could. Claudius Rufus could answer any prayer, cast any spell, with his Book of Necromancy. Martius only need take me to the Temple of Venus. I could become mortal again. I could regain human status. And once I was made whole, I would help Julia to escape, perhaps even escape with her. Either that, or Julia could become my handmaiden if I went to live with Martius in the Gladiators' Quarters. Gathering all my courage, I told Martius about my life and death. It was the night of August 21 (AD 79).

We had just made the best love any couple could ever experience. As usual, Julia had licked me and touched me and readied me for his maleness. After Martius' fourth orgasm, while we lay in each other's arms, I said, "There is something I must tell you."

"What, my love?" he inquired softly.

"I am not of this world."

"I know that, my love. You are an angel. A wonderful beautiful angel. My angel."

"No. You do not understand. I am not an angel. I am a girl who died of fever and was entombed, only to be brought here two days later, after Claudius Rufus at the Temple of Venus worked his spell. I can only remain here for twenty-one days. Then, I am to be burned in the secret crematorium that resides within the House of Cryptoporticus. I am undead."

Martius just looked at me, shocked. For an instant, he said nothing. Then, he rose, a serious stunned look on his face and walked silently from the brothel. I did not see him again for three days. Time was running out for Julia. Tomorrow she would die unless I intervened.

I could bear it no longer. I would go to the Temple of Venus myself. I would beg Claudius Rufus to make me whole. *If I am whole and human, Martius cannot fail to love me once again, and he will help us,* I thought.

I decided to make my escape in the early hours of the afternoon, before the men began to come after dark. I tiptoed stealthily from the brothel and out into the street. I must go north, towards the Porta di Sarino. I would come to the House of Venus. Claudius Rufus would work his magic on my decomposing form. After I was transformed, I would continue towards the Amphitheatre and the Arcaded Court of the Gladiators nearby, where Martius resided. Martius would rejoice in my newfound health and wholeness. *He will love me again, and I will make him happy. He will help me, and I can come back and help Julia escape her fate*

The pebbles beneath my bare feet cut deeply into the soles of my feet. Prostitutes in Pompeii have no opportunities to go outside. I had no shoes, no sandals. We spent most of our time in the brothel toughening our souls, to be able to deal with a never-ending succession of strangers who raped us, over and over again. Only I had escaped such a fate, because Martius paid Sittius handsomely for my exclusive services. But Martius' money would soon run out. Other men would then come. If not that, my twenty-one days would expire, and I would be escorted to the crematorium for a more final solution. I could not afford to wait any longer. I must act alone.

Just then, a huge explosion shook the world. Mt. Vesuvius hurled fireballs from the depths of its chasm. Magma and lava flowed from the now active volcano and volcanic ash blackened the sunny sky, a black river of ash and lapilli that came from the crater and ran throughout the city, completely blacking out the sun. It was August 24 (79AD).

As I had gone such a little way, I first tried to return to the brothel for shelter. Nearing the garden beneath my window, I heard the voice of Sittius saying, to the guards, "If she returns, seize her and we will take her to the crematorium immediately." Upon hearing this, I fled in the opposite direction, toward the Amphitheater and the Arcaded Court of the Gladiators, where the gladiators trained and lived. I would find Martius. We would go to the Temple of Venus together and beg Claudius Rufus to make me whole.

As I neared the Arcaded Court of the Gladiators, I stumbled into Martius. *He must be coming to rescue me*, I thought. *He does love me.* The ash was now so thick that we could barely speak. We coughed and joined hands.

"Please," I whispered. "Go with me to the Temple of Venus. Go with me to see Claudius Rufus. He can cure me. Using the Book of Necromancy, he can bring me back to life. I will be made whole again."

Martius was coughing too hard for speech, but he managed to choke out, "Take my hand." I took the hand of the only lover I had ever known, the only man I had ever lain with, the man I trusted above all others. We ran away from the ash, towards the Temple of Venus. After just a few steps, Martius stopped and said, "We have to go back. We are going the wrong way. Claudius Rufus lives yonder." Martius pointed towards the mouth of hell, the gaping maw of flowing lava and fire that was the erupting volcano Mt. Vesuvius.

"Are you sure?"

"Yes, I'm sure. We need to go that way." Martius took a firm grip of my hand again, and we ran swiftly against the wind and darkness. The wind carried death in its arms. The ash raining down on us brought total destruction for the 10,000 doomed inhabitants of Pompeii.

When we had run until I could run no more, the rim of the volcano loomed.

"Martius…we must go in the opposite direction. We are too close to the volcano. Surely Claudius Rufus has fled to the Temple of Venus. He would want to save the sacred books. He would want to flee the danger, as we do."

"I want to flee the danger, Livia, " said Martius, lifting me in his arms, "but the danger is you, you undead monster." With these hateful words, Martius flung me towards the very mouth of the blazing volcano, toward the depths of hell.

The burning. The pain. The flesh melting from my bones. I experienced everything I had feared and more. It was worse than my nightmares of the crematorium. I felt more pain emotionally, realizing that it was by the hand of Martius Titienses, my love. He was the only man I had ever loved, and he had betrayed me.

As I thought I was about to be consumed by the flames, in agony, plunged into eternal grief , I experienced conflicting emotions and a moment of hope like a flickering flame, a beacon beckoning me to a safe place beyond the pain of my brief days on Earth. There, behind Martius stood Julia. She had followed me when I returned to the brothel. She cradled a heavy rock in her hands and, just as Martius was about to shove me further into the flowing lava pit, Julia brought the boulder down upon Martius' head. It was not a glancing blow. It was a killing blow that he never saw coming. Julia grabbed my hand, pulled me from the river of lava.

"Follow me. Quickly," Julia said.

As Martius had held me in his arms during the deep bruise of night, I had whispered to him, *"Once I love someone, my love remains constant. I love you now, and I will love you forever. Love never dies."* When Julia kissed me softly and brought me to climax, to prepare me for love-making, I had whispered the same message to her.

Julia and I ran as quickly as we could away from the volcano. We tried desperately to flee the scene of Julia's murder of Martius and her selfless rescue of me. But I was badly burned and limping and we were no more fortunate than the other ten thousand doomed inhabitants of Pompeii. Out of breath, in pain from my burns, we crawled beneath a stairwell of a nearby villa, hiding from anyone who might have seen Julia's crime, gasping for air, cradling one another as the oxygen was consumed by the volcano's flames. The silt-like ash settled on our forms. We curled, spoon-like beneath the staircase. Julia and I realized that we were going to die a second time, but at least we would die together.

Something even more important dawned on me. My love for Martius did not die, even though he had flung me into the depths of Hell. And, as I faced my ultimate fate with Julia in my arms and I in hers, I knew, more than ever, that my words were true: *Love never dies.*

Konerak

KONERAK QUIVERED. *Beast come back. No more! No more cut Konerak!*

The cold tile of the bathroom wall. Blood inside the tub, Konerak's blood.

The tall blonde man opened the bathroom door, approached Konerak.

"This won't hurt. Prince Philip of Orange had it done seventeen times by his surgeon. Nearly everyone lives. Well, 70%, anyway. It won't hurt... too much. There aren't that many nerves in your skull. After I bore the hole, I'll put in a nice soothing medicine. You'll heal up and be as good as new."

Jeffrey busied himself sharpening the ancient instrument, one used in Hippocrates' time. "One French doc...he drilled 52 holes in a patient's head in just 2 months. The man lived. So, don't worry. This will help you to accept your new life. I'm not such a bad guy. When you tried to get away and ran out into the street, that was stupid. Don't do that again, or I *will* kill you. I told those cops we were lovers. We *will* be lovers. You will stay with me."

Konerak did not understand a single word. Konerak was of the Hmong people of Laos. The Hmong didn't have a written language for centuries, only receiving one (courtesy of well-meaning missionaries and Shong Lue Yang) in 1959. Although Konerak grew up in the Xieng Khouang Province, he learned neither French nor English. Working to grow melons and beans and corn and yams to eat, and opium poppies to sell was his clan's life. Slash and burn farming in the foothills and mountains of southern China and, eventually, in Laos. He'd only been in Milwaukee for six months.

Slash and burn. If Konerak had known the meaning of those English words, he would now be able to relate to them in terms of what was happening to him in Jeffrey's apartment tub.

How I get here? Konerak wondered. He remembered very little of the night, three days earlier. A bar. Loud music. Drink. Much cash. The man looked nice. *I think he want sex, for money.* Konerak's slight build made him a frequent target in gay bars. American men would pay well for services.

Konerak had broken out of the apartment, wandered, dazed into the streets, until the cops found him. The Beast was right behind him. Konerak did not know the language of the policemen. They returned him to the white devil. Now, Konerak lay in the bloody bathtub, trussed, cut, bleeding, terrified.

Konerak tried to summon the strength to pull away from the sharp pointed instrument that Jeffrey held in his hands, but he was weak, both from loss of blood and from torture. He stank from urine and feces and blood and fear. He shook his head from side to side: *No! No! No! No!* Eyes wide with fear.

The beast approached his head with a drill.

"I'm just going to take a small piece out of your skull, now," said Jeffrey in what Jeffrey hoped was a soothing voice. "I'll grind it up and drink it in my coffee." A weird smile. "The Incas thought it would make your spirit strong. Then, I'm going to pour this nice medicine (Jeffrey motioned towards a brown bottle on the floor) in the hole, and you'll be fine. And we'll be friends…and more." Jeffrey smiled. "Are you OK with that?"

Konerak was not okay with that. He was far from okay with that.

I son of Shaman. You no cut son of Shaman. Hmong Ntsuab cannibals. I not cannibal. I white Hmong.

Despite the excruciating pain and the frequent blackouts from the pain, Konerak was praying to his god, Dab Phuaj Thaub, the Mountain God. He was thinking of his brave Grandfather, General Vang Pao. Hmong means "free men." Konerak knew that his people had fought against Chinese oppression from 3000 BC until the 16th century; he was one with his people. He would fight to be free.

General Vang Pao led 7,000 Hmong mountain volunteers against the Viet Cong for the United States during the Vietnam War. It was "a secret war," one that the United States refused to acknowledge for years. Colonel Arthur "Bull" Simon and the Army's 77th Special Forces White Star team came to Xeng Khouang Province in the mountains, atop the 4,500 foot

Padong mountain overlooking the Plaine des Jarres, where Konerak grew up. Others, in Laos, located atop Phou Bia, the highest and least accessible mountain peak in Laos, rallied by spiritual leader Zong Zoua Her, were encouraged to block the Ho Chi Minh Trail, the main military supply route from the north to the south. The Hmong also rescued downed American pilots. More than 40,000 Hmong were killed in the front lines. Over 80% of the Hmong men in Laos were recruited by the CIA to fight the Secret War. Hmong suffered a very high casualty rate…countless men missing in action, thousands more injured or disabled. The Hmong, descendants of the Mongols, always faced fear with bravery.

Konerak was just a boy when Vang Pao led his rag-tag band of guerilla fighters in forming the first-line of infantry defense and attack against the enemy. General Vang Pao led Region II (MR2) against NVA incursion from headquarters in Long Cheng (Lima Site 20). For a while, Long Cheng was the second largest city in Laos, with 300,000 people, among them 200,000 ethnic Hmong. Long Chen was a micro-nation. It had a bank, an airport, a school system, officials, and military units. But Long Cheng fell in and out of General Vang Pao's control. Konerak never received any schooling, as he was not the one in his family selected to be so favored. He was better suited to watch his Shaman father and learn how to heal, and to work days planting and harvesting the staple crops the clan needed for sustenance.

Once, Konerak remembered, he saw his Grandfather Vang Pao supervising the interrogation of two informants, an old man and a younger man. Both prisoners were tied up. They sat, terrified, just as he was now, in a corner of a thatched bamboo hut at Lima Site 20. Konerak had seen them, as he brought water for his Grandfather and his Grandfather's men. Soon, his Grandfather released the old man, who pleaded for his life in fluent but frequently unintelligible words of the White Hmong. Then, with the exclamation "Ba!" the younger man was taken outside. Four shots rang out. When Konerak left the hut, the young man's body lay in the dust, his eyes wide in death, blood seeping from a bullet wound to his head just above his left ear. The force of the bullet had removed much of the rest of the young man's skull. Now, the young man was just a spirit, left to wander the mountains. A lump of clay. He would have no life beyond his life on this earth. He would commune with no spirits, father no children, wear no ceremonial headgear, play no Ncas, the courtship mouth harp that made the eerie noise. He would not take part in the ball ceremony, using the ball to select a maiden to be his wife. He was just dead.

Konerak did not want his life to end in this fashion. He would need to draw on the spirit of his ancestors and try to remember things that he had intentionally forgotten, in order to assimilate with his Wisconsin neighbors. Now, he needed the wisdom of the ancients, wisdom he had watched in action when he was just a lad of six. *Could he remember what he had seen done by his Shaman father? Would it work? Was there a little of his Grandfather, General Vang Pao, that would guide him in his fight?*

Now it was Konerak who was suffering from a wound to his head, a painful, agonizing wound, but it did not stop him from thinking, from communing with his ancestors, from asking his father, the Shaman, to guide him in his struggle to survive.

His Grandfather Pao always said that Konerak's body, like his father's before him, hosted a "neng", a healing spirit. Konerak remembered watching his father, the respected Shaman of his clan, go into a deep trance to commune with spirits of the dead. The spirits would tell him what must be done to heal his patients. He would use his cymbal, (the Nruas neeb) or his scissors (Rab txiab) and chanting sounds accompanied the cymbal.

I must remember the chant. I must remember the chant.

The Whistle of Death. Konerak remembered the Whistle of Death. A sound his father could make that would drive the evil spirits away. The sound would render the evil spirits useless, would heal the afflicted villagers who came to him with their many ailments.

Can I commune with the spirits of my ancestors now, with my god of the mountains, Dab Phuaj Thaub, and ask this god to help me to use the Whistle of Death? If I channel the "neng," I can live.

All Konerak wanted to do was to live and love and have a life. He asked for very little from life. After months and then years spent in the relocation camps of Nong Khai and Ban Vanui and Bee Thao, Konerak had come to America. He was alone, sponsored only by a church group. His mother, uncle and father had all died in the crossing of the Mekong River and the small boy had spent years, growing to young adulthood in the never-changing ennui of the refugee camps. Nothing to do. No crops to tend. No work for the men. No education for the children.

Sometimes, they were shown Disney movies on a giant outdoor screen. Most did not understand the dialogue, but they knew Mickey Mouse and Goofy and other Disney characters. All the young children huddled together under the starry sky, watching the American cartoon characters and wondering what had become of their mothers, their fathers, their entire families, their clan. It was a sad and difficult time, but

Konerak had emerged from the camps, at 18, and had been sent to California, where, once again, he spent time in a relocation camp until the Church of Saint Sabina sent for him to come live in Milwaukee and work as a bus boy in a restaurant.

Even this simple job was a challenge, as Konerak worked to learn the language of the Americans. It had not been necessary to learn to speak English in Nong Khai or Ban Vanui or Bee Thao, but it was necessary in California and in Wisconsin. And, since Konerak had never learned an alphabet or had formal education in his own homeland or in any language, it made learning English that much more difficult. He was still struggling with the task when he met Jeffrey in the bar that night three days ago, which seemed more like three years ago, now.

After so many years, it was difficult for Konerak to remember all the rituals Konerak's Shaman father had used, but, he thought, *I must try*. When Konerak had left the Province and crossed the Mekong River into Thailand with his family, he was only a small six-year-old boy. The Hmong were targeted for retaliation after U.S. withdrawal from Vietnam in 1975. The Hmong guerilla fighters had helped the white devils. When the Communists overthrew the Lao kingdom, there was massive retaliation against them, as, indeed, there had been against the Hmong for centuries for one reason or another.

The fall-out from helping the United States in Vietnam was worse, even, then the persecution the Hmong had faced in 1920, when they revolted against the colonial authorities, the French, in "La Guerre des Fous," the War of the Insane. The Hmong called the war Rog Paj Cai, after their brave leader Paj Cai who led them. In Hmong, the war was called The War of the Flowering of the Law. To the French, the Hmong were insane to revolt, insane to try to overthrow the French and drive them from Indochina, and, ultimately, insane to help the Americans in fighting along the Ho Chi Minh trail. Konerak thought he was now experiencing true insanity in Jeffrey's squalid Milwaukee apartment.

A mass exodus of Hmong people from Laos ensued. Konerak and his mother Phia Chang, and his father, Doua Vang, and his uncle, Yo Moua, had fled together. Four of them in a small rowboat, trying to cross the Mekong River at midnight

My mother...she shot crossing the river...My uncle die in boat. Many bullets fly over our heads. I crouch in bottom of the boat. My mother shield me with body. She say, "Do not look up. Live to tell others." When we reach other side, my mother dead. Uncle die, too. Konerak, alone, survive. Kon-

erak must live to tell others. Mother say, Remember you Hmong: fighter for freedom always.

The thought made Konerak struggle again against the bungee cords that bound him.

Konerak saw the small brown bottle that Jeffrey had brought to the edge of the tub. Its cap had been removed and it sat there, glinting in the dim light of the bathroom. Jeffrey had told Konerak that the bottle contained a soothing ointment, but, in the glass lip of the bottle, Konerak saw an opportunity.

He remembered his father's use of the Whistle of Death to drive out evil demons. His father would blow on an object made of clay and molded into a small instrument that looked a bit like an ocarina. Konerak had no such instrument, but he remembered the keening sound, the piercing noise that the Whistle of Death made. Before cannibalistic rituals, some said, the Whistle of Death was used before the victims were killed. Konerak had been in the United States long enough to know that one could make an eerily similar noise by blowing on the lip of a beer bottle. Hmong, after all, are naturally musical, playing instruments at weddings, crafting the batik sewing patterns, Paj ntuab quuj.

Konerak could make this sound, this keening sound of the "geez" player of his people, although he would have to improvise. He would summon his ancestors. He would summon the dead of his clan, a proud band of fighters to the death, to help him against the Beast who now tortured him without cause.

Konerak's eyes glazed over. Excruciating pain rendered him stuporous; his gag was loose, and he soon scraped it from his face.

Before the Beast had placed the gag loosely over his mouth, Konerak had pleaded with him in broken English, *Konerak not do anything bad. Please! Please! Please!*

Konerak was not pleading any more. Now, Konerak would fight, like his grandfather, who had been called the Wizard of Oz by the Americans, or Uncle by his own people, or the Vice President of Oz. He would combine the strength of General Vang Pao and the secret knowledge of his own Shaman father, Doua Vang, and, together with his human desire to live, he would harness the healing inner spirit of "neng" and commune with those who had crossed over. Pain is always a teacher. It teaches you about your own humanity. It teaches you how much you can endure and still triumph. Pain was the great teacher for Konerak, now, alone and defenseless in Jeffrey's tub, in Jeffrey's apartment, in the foreign land of Milwaukee, Wisconsin.

What must I do, Oh, Ancient Ones? He struggled to divine their response, sent to him telepathically as he lapsed into a near trance. He sensed dimly shrouded figures. His mother. His uncle. His father. Others he did not know. He felt them all sending him their energy. He sensed it through the excruciating pain.

You must chant the chant and make the sound of the Whistle of Death. This was his father, Doua Vang, speaking from beyond the grave, his visage ringed by the clouds that once nestled atop the mountaintops of their Laotian homeland.

How can I make the sound? I have no Paj ntuab quuz. I have no geez. I have no musical instruments. I have no Whistle of Death.

Konerak knew, in his heart, what the answer would be.

Use the lip of the brown bottle. Reach it now. Chant. Blow. You can do it. Your ancestors conquered all of China under the Ming Dynasty. You can overcome the Beast. You are Konerak of the Vang clan. You are invincible. You are free man and will fight to the death to remain free man. We will help you in your fight against the Beast.

Konerak slowly and quietly shifted his weight to the edge of the tub, leaning over the cold porcelain lip of the old-fashioned, claw-footed bathtub to place his bleeding lips on the edge of the open brown bottle of medicine that Jeffrey had left there on the floor when the phone rang. He also began chanting, under his breath, the ancient chant he had heard his father use to drive the evil spirits from the sick.

Kia Vue, Mee Vue, Nao Kao Xiong. Kia Vue, Mee Vue, Nao KaoXiong.

The chant grew in intensity as Konerak gathered all his inner strength to reach the lip of the brown bottle and to use it as his father had used the Whistle of Death before him in the days of old. Soon, Konerak was chanting repeatedly, as quickly as possible, and he reached the bottle and blew across the lip of the vial, still sitting where Jeffrey had left it on the floor near the tub.

The sound was piercing. It was keening. It was inhuman. It was strange and bizarre and eerie, and the screaming and shrieking that Konerak heard coming from the other room was otherworldly.

After a long time, Konerak heard noises in the outer room. Neighbors pounded on the door. Police had been summoned. The sound of the door being broken was music to Konerak's ears.

Later, when the police asked Konerak what had happened to Jeffrey, who was found with a frozen death grimace and a look of horror on his face in the living room, Konerak just shook his head.

I not know. I prisoner.

Police soon gave up trying to question the young man. He was obviously out of his mind. After a hospital stay, Konerak was released. (No insurance dictated a quick overnight stay.)

Yes, thought Konerak, *I out of mind. I in mind of Hmong ancestors. Thank you, oh mighty Wizard of Oz. Thank you, oh beloved father. I Shaman now. Konerak will tell others of your lives.*

Effie, We Hardly Knew Ye!

"GIVE ME A SHAVE, EFFIE," the patient said to the attentive nurse sponge-bathing him in his hospital bed.

"Now, Bill. You know my name's not Effie. I'm Lucy." The nurse continued washing the injured 84-year-old, who, even though he lay dying, constantly made passes at all the pretty nurses. Lucy smiled indulgently at the old man.

"As soon as I get out of this damn-fool place, I'm gonna' take you out for a night on the town," said William B. Skirvin, oil-rich millionaire and owner of the Skirvin Hotel in Oklahoma City, Oklahoma. He coughed and blood from his lungs joined sputum in the handkerchief with which Lucy wiped his mouth. Maybe not. Two weeks later, William B. Skirvin was dead.

W.B. Skirvin didn't take Lucy out on the town before he died. Shortly after that exchange with his nurse, two weeks after a car crash that threw him through the windshield of Earl Saxon's car as they headed west along NW63 in Oklahoma City and were cut off by a hit-and-run driver who forced them off the road and into a creek bed near Grand Boulevard, W.B. Skirvin—the seemingly indestructible oil millionaire—was dead.

W.B., a farm-implement salesman from Michigan, had single-handedly created a new town, Alta Loma, 18 miles north of Galveston, simply by showing pictures of a big red strawberry to neighbors in frozen Michigan in the dead of winter and inviting them to come enjoy "the sunshine in Texas." W.B. made his money striking oil in places like Spindletop. And he made lots of it. But W.B. Skirvin was dead before he could take Lucy out dancing, or make amends for his dead mistress, Effie.

45

W.B. could sell anything to anyone. He sold the biggest bill of goods to Effie Waterman (not her real name), a maid in his showcase hotel in downtown Oklahoma City at One Park Avenue and Broadway. Effie was a pretty thing half his age.

"Effie…you know I'm lonely, honey. A man has needs. My wife, Hattie's, been dead for years now. A man has needs."

"But…W.B. Will you take care of me? I mean, after? Will you respect me and take care of me?" The pretty brunette looked fetching in her maid's uniform, but dubious about her employer's proposition.

"Sure I will. Effie…you know me. Have I ever been anything but good to you? Of course, I'll take care of you!"

And so it was that Effie Waterman became the mistress of one of the richest men in Oklahoma City, a man who had built the grandest hotel in all of Oklahoma, a man four times her age, and a hotel that W.B.'s famous daughter, Perle Mesta referred to as "Father's 300-room hobby." W.B. was constantly adding floors to the hotel. When it opened in 1911, it was two 10-story towers and featured imported Austrian chandeliers in the lobby. Price tag: $10,000 per chandelier. When Perle was named Ambassadress to Luxembourg and began being called "the hostess with the mostest," because of her lavish Washington, D.C., parties, she also brought attention to W.B.'s masterpiece, the Skirvin Hotel in Oklahoma City. The play "Call Me Madam" was based on Perle's life.

It was probably inevitable that the now-famous Perle and her equally strong-willed Dad would eventually clash. In 1930, W.B. added more floors, until the hotel was fourteen stories high. Perle didn't like that. "The General," as W.B. called her, wanted the money Dad used on expanding the hotel to be used, instead, to drill for more oil. The pair had invested together in oil fields in Oklahoma City in 1930 and had discovered wells that had the potential to produce up to 40,000 barrels a day. But, in 1944, W.B. wanted to build another twenty-eight-story tower for his masterpiece, the Skirvin Hotel. Perle thought this was just pure foolishness. She convinced her sister Marguerite and her brother William of it, as well, but it was Perle who lodged the first lawsuit to remove W.B. from managing his own affairs.

Prohibition was in full swing when Effie became pregnant with W.B.'s illegitimate child. W.B. had promised to "take care" of Effie. He imported a mid-wife to deliver the child in the hotel. Best to keep any breath of scandal away from friends and family. It wouldn't do to have Oklahoma City know about his mistress and their child.

"You know I'll take good care of you and the baby, Effie. Didn't I promise to take care of you? Have the little one and I'll put you up in the penthouse of the hotel." W.B. beamed at his own generosity, his teeth clenched tightly on his ever-present cigar, and Effie…who had come to really love the old man…. smiled back, a small, grateful smile.

Effie, a chambermaid of modest means from a family of humble origins, was overwhelmed at the thought of actually living in the penthouse with the spectacular view, the corner suite that overlooked Park Avenue and Broadway. It was a massive room with dark mahogany wainscoting, dark wood floors, and a fantastic view of the city below. One of the expensive chandeliers of Austrian crystal, like those in the lobby, was a highlight of the multi-room penthouse.

So, Effie Waterman bore W.B. Skirvin's daughter in the penthouse, with a private mid-wife supervising. Effie was hidden from view on the 14th-floor penthouse of W.B.'s grand hotel. Or his "grand hobby", if you cared to use the term used by his daughters, Perle and Marguerite, and his son, William.

Although there were whispers of W.B.'s bastard child, W.B. made it clear to Effie that she must stay in the penthouse, in order to keep their relationship and their child a secret.

"But…W.B.…the baby is walking now. Little Effie's never been outside. She deserves to feel the sun on her face. Maybe even to get to know her half-sisters and half-brothers? Sooner or later, she must go to school."

When W.B. heard these ideas, he instantly secured security guards to constantly stand guard outside the penthouse doors. They made sure that Effie Waterman didn't wander off or reveal the secret they had agreed to share.

"Now, honey. You know we can't have Perle and Marguerite and William getting all riled up about you and the baby?"

"Why not? What's wrong with me? What's wrong with Little Effie? Don't you love us?"

"Of course I do, darlin', but it wouldn't do to give Perle and Marguerite and William any ammunition to fight me with. I intend to expand the hotel again…this time with a new tower across Broadway…and Perle doesn't want me to. She wants me to keep drillin' for oil in Oklahoma. Ah! You'll see. The hotel'll be grand and you'll have the catbird's seat…a bird's-eye view from the penthouse. It's going to be a 28-story tower. This will be the best damned hotel in the Midwest. Hell! It'll be the best damned hotel in the whole United States of America! And you'll be part of it, because, you see, I want you to stay here in the hotel with me. You're livin' in the lap of luxury. The top floor penthouse of the best hotel in the country. Do you want for anything? Aren't you well fed, well housed? Aren't you treated well?"

"But I'm lonely, W.B.…."

"Lonely! Pshaw! That's no big deal. You know I'll come visit you."

"Yes, you'll come, but I don't get to go out. I don't get to see my mother, my father, my friends. I don't ever get to leave. The baby never gets to leave."

"Darling, you're just a little unhinged about having a baby. That's all. It happens to women all the time, especially women as young as you." W.B.'s withered old hand stroked her pink youthful cheek.

"No, W.B. Little Effie is almost a year old, and I haven't been allowed to leave the penthouse in all that time." Effie repeated this complaint whenever W.B visited.

This familiar refrain played out over and over during W.B. Skirvin's clandestine visits to Effie, until, one day, he forbade her to speak of it to him.

"Honey, you know you can't go gallivanting around just now. Marguerite and Perle and William are fighting me for control. If they know about you…" W.B. left the statement unfinished, but Effie understood. She looked ineffably sad. The next day, Effie and Little Effie were dead. Distraught, unhappy, alone, isolated from her family and friends, Effie Waterman clutched her small daughter to her breast and jumped from the fourteenth floor penthouse window to the pavement below. No newspaper in Oklahoma City printed the details of the death of W.B.'s mistress and illegitimate child.

Legal battles strained the family relations in 1949, when Perle Mesta, W.B.'s daughter, who had married wealthy businessman George Mesta, filed a lawsuit in the 10th. U.S. Circuit Court of Appeals, trying to oust her father from the managing of the hotel and from running his own affairs. Marguerite had also returned home by that point in time, after dropping a career as a stage and screen actress. Marguerite married Robert Adams and returned to live in the Skirvin Hotel for several years with her daughter, Betty. It was Marguerite's presence in the hotel that made W.B. especially careful not to let Effie or Little Effie fly away from the love nest he had made for them.

On March 11, 1944, the 10th U.S. Circuit judge ruled that W.B. Skirvin was as mentally sharp as ever, and completely competent to manage his 300-room hotel, if he wished to do so, which quelled the mutiny of W.B.'s legitimate heirs. After all, said the judge in defending W.B. against charges of mis-management that led to hotel losses, the entire economy was depressed throughout the 1930's, not just Oklahoma City and the Skirvin Hotel. The judge also said, "You Skirvins ought to be ashamed of yourselves!"

It's not known if the judge was referring to the death of Effie, which had taken place shortly before this. The local press had buried that story. Perhaps the judge found the fight over W.B. Skirvin's assets, while W.B. was still alive and well, unseemly. The judge said, in ruling for W.B. and against Perle and her brother and sister, "Age alone of an owner or manager of a property is not enough to warrant the appointment of a receiver or the continuation of an existing receivership. W.B. Skirvin is more than 80 years of age and if the properties are restored by their owners, he may again become the active manager."

As W.B. Skirvin lay dying...consumed by guilt over his dead mistress and child, who had succumbed to the loneliness and isolation he had imposed upon them in their penthouse prison....W.B. said, to his three children, "I've forgiven you. There's nothing but love in my heart for all three of you children; you're all I have."

W.B. might have added, "You're the only children I have *now*. Now that Effie and Little Effie are dead."

Ever since that day, guests at the hotel have seen maids' carts move mysteriously down the hall, no human in sight. Guests have heard voices: the crying of a woman and a child. One male guest said he heard a woman outside his bathroom shower door saying, "Can I come in and be with you? I'm so lonely. Can I join you, please?" He was afraid to come out of the shower!

Guests of the Skirvin Hotel continued to hear the mysterious crying of a woman and a child after Effie's death until the hotel closed in 1988. There were continued reports of maids' carts moving mysteriously in the hallways, unattended by live maids...especially on the fourteenth floor. Men would sometimes see a naked woman in their shower or hear a soft female voice crying, whimpering, begging for company. Small children heard the voice of another little girl crying inconsolably.

The strains of the fabled parties of "the hostess with the mostest" have long given way to cries of despair and betrayal from Effie and her daughter, the woman who was Perle Mesta's half-sister, in life, and the child who was her niece. May they rest in peace.

Circle Three: Gluttony

IN THE STRANGE STORY of "Amazing Andy, the Wonder Chicken," it is Mama's gluttony that sets everything in motion.

Based on the true story of "Miracle Mike," the fictional "Mama" proves to be a glutton in more ways than one.

Amazing Andy, the Wonder Chicken

MAMA HAS ALWAYS HAD A LOVE for other people's possessions. That's why, when she came over for a fine fried chicken dinner with Stanley and me that Sunday, we knew she'd want all the best parts of the bird.

"Now, Stanley," she said, "when you go to killin' that there chicken be sure to leave a generous neck bone. You know how much I like the neck bone." Mama licked her lips in anticipation and smiled her best loving mother-in-law smile at Stan, who was only too pleased to do her bidding.

"Indeed I do, Winnie," said Stanley, returning her grin with his best son-in-law smile. He walked out the door, axe in hand, whistling.

Stanley Carlsen later said, with a pout, "It was as important to suck up to your mother-in-law in the 1940's as it is today. But who knew that suckin' up to Winnie didn't mean that she was gonna' feel any loyalty to you down the line?" Stan was definitely planning on sucking up to Winnie as much as possible. He was going to start by killing that two and one-half pound Wyandotte rooster for Sunday dinner.

As a general rule, Stanley Carlsen always aimed to please. Only problem was, this time Stan's aim must have been off, because there were unintended consequences of Stan's October 10th, 1945, chicken-killing. Unintended in more ways than one.

While tryin' to cut off Andy's head in such a way as to leave a generous neck bone for Winnie, Stan managed to remove most of Andy's head, which he later placed in a jar. The chicken's brain stem and one ear remained attached. Most of a chicken's reflex actions are controlled by the brain stem. Chickens as animals are dumb as dirt. They'll stand in the rain lookin' up till they drown, so our chicken seemed just as smart *after* he lost his head as he did *before*. And he was, for sure, just as healthy; his weight quadrupled in eighteen months' time.

"Shit! I missed the jugular!" exclaimed Stanley. "Girls! Come on out here and take a look at this ol' bird! There must be a blood clot or some-thin', or he'd be bleedin' to death."

Stanley looked ruefully at the chicken, which was, indeed, running around like a chicken with its head cut off. Amazing Andy, as he came to be called, was not bleedin' much, either. There are just some things in life that happen and you can't explain 'em; you really don't plan for 'em to happen, but they do.

Mama and me heard the commotion outside. We joined Stan in the yard when he hollered. There was Stan, bloody axe in hand, standin' by the stump we used for killin' chickens. In the background was this bloody headless chicken, runnin' from our back yard to the neighbors', flappin' its wings fit to kill. Blood spouting from its neck was spattering the catalpa tree blossoms in the neighbors' yard, giving the lawn the appearance of some kind of colorful crazy quilt sewn by a drunken seamstress.

"What-the-hell is goin' on, Stanley?" I screamed. I've been Stan's wife for twenty-five years. Never, in all those years, have I got used to watchin' any animal be butchered, whether it's a chicken or a hog or a cow.

"Well, Mabel. I don't rightly know what to tell you, but I ain't gonna' kill this here particular rooster. I tried, but he seems to be more like a cat with nine lives. I don't think I can bring myself to killin' him, now. I been sayin', 'It's a miracle! It's a miracle!' I think this rooster deserves a reprieve. I'm callin' this lucky devil Amazing Andy, the Wonder Chicken. I'll just have to kill us some other chicken for dinner tonight."

Stanley also got me and Mama into the act of helpin' feed Andy with an eye-dropper, since Andy didn't have no head and all. We had to make sure to keep his esophagus clear and give him grain and water, but, other than that, Andy put on weight. He weighed eight pounds before you knew it. I'd say he had an eye for the ladies, 'cept he didn't have no eyes at all. The ladies…chickens, I mean…liked him just fine. He was always in there doin' his thing in the hen house. Andy was a fine specimen of a chicken, if there ever was one.

Seein' Andy headin' for the hen house for the tenth time that day, Mama said, "That Andy sure proves that just because you're handicapped don't mean you can't have a good fulfillin' life." We agreed with her. The trouble hadn't started yet.

Word got around quick that we had us a chicken with no head that was livin' with the other chickens in our backyard in Boonesville, servicin' the hens in the hen house and just generally actin' normal. [As normal as you can act when you don't have no head, that is]. Crowin' early in the mornin' was out, of course. It's hard to crow when your head sits in a jar by the door, but Andy had never been much of a crower, anyways.

Pretty soon the town reporter, Gayle Begley, came out from the *Boonesville Times* to do a story on Andy, just like they done on Farmer Whitlock's two-headed calf the year before. Soon after that, we was gettin' offers for interviews from *Time* and *Life* and they was callin' Andy "The Wonder Chicken." Then someone suggested the tour. Times was tough, and it seemed like a good idea.

We took out an insurance policy for $10,000 on Andy and hit the road. New York. Atlantic City. Los Angeles. San Diego. We took Andy to Salt Lake City, up to the University there, about two hundred and fifty miles away, where the animal doctors explained how it's possible for a live chicken with no head to survive. They was amazed at how healthy ol' Andy was. That kind of took the wind out of the sails of the animal rights people, who'd been tryin' to stir up a fuss. No chicken had ever seemed happier than Amazing Andy, the Wonder Chicken, and, on top of that, people was willin' to pay good hard-earned cash to see him, at a time when cash was in short supply.

That's when the trouble started.

First, Mama said she'd like to have Andy sleep in her room at night, while we were on the road. "Just to make sure he's all right," she said. This seemed kind of dumb, since it was because of Mama that Andy had no head in the first place. But me and Stan humored her, since, after all, she *was* helpin' us keep the books and helpin' feed Andy with the eye-dropper and just generally goin' along with us on the trip across the country, which was quite lucrative, as headless chicken tours go.

It wasn't until we got to Chicago that we noticed that there was money missin' from Andy's bank deposit bag.

"Mama, " I said, "have you seen the money bag with Andy's money in it?" Mama didn't answer, but I knew right away from the look on her face that she'd taken it.

"Why, no, Baby. I don't know nothin' about no money." Mama was pretendin' to be readin' the good book in her room, with Andy runnin' around underneath her feet. I could always tell when Mama was lyin'. Ever since Daddy ran off with Hazel Williamson and Mama told me that "the angels had taken him," I'd been able to spot her lyin' from a mile away. Mama was lyin' now.

We started to watch Mama close, since Mama has always had a love for other people's possessions. And Amazing Andy the Wonder Chicken was *our* chicken, whether he had escaped bein' her Sunday dinner or not. And Amazing Andy's money was *our* money. Not Mama's.

Except that Mama didn't see it that way.

Things started to get real weird after that. We was barely speakin' when we finally got close to home, after the big Grand Tour. Thousands of dollars we shoulda' had from Andy's tour had dwindled to whatever we were able to salvage from the point when we found out Mama was robbin' us, till we got home to the farm in Boonesville. We only had a couple hundred dollars left, by then. Lord knows what Winnie did with it.

Stanley said, "It just ain't right. Family is family. After all we done for Mama, it just ain't right." He twisted his weather-beaten John Deere cap in his hands as he said this, and he didn't look at all happy. Stan hadn't been sleeping sound like he used to, either. Used to be, as soon as his head hit the pillow, he was out as quick as a bee sting, but, since the trouble, he seemed restless and jumpy. I didn't know what to say to comfort him, 'cause he did have a point, after all.

I was sleepin' hard one night just after we got back, and it was way after midnight. The smell of lilac was in the air and it sorta' sounded like somebody was movin' furniture around in my living room, when I half-heard a commotion from the yard. Shades of October tenth, if I didn't think, half asleep like I was, that Stan was out there killin' us another chicken. I heard the sound of the axe on the stump. I could almost see the blood flyin'.

There was screamin', though, Chickens don't scream when you're killin' them with an axe. They just flap their wings and run around with blood flyin' off their severed necks. Except for Amazing Andy, the Wonder Chicken, that is. But miracle chickens like Andy don't come down the pike every day.

And Mama? A chicken can live without its head. But a grown 210-pound female?

Not a chance.

Circle Four: Hoarders & Wasters

AS WE ENTER THE FOURTH CIRCLE OF HELL, we encounter all those who hoarded and/or wasted material goods during life.

A family that brought lager beer to the city of St. Louis had
its share of wastrels, and then there's the Queen Bee…

The Lemp Mansion Curse

JOHANN ADAM LEMP OF ESCHWEGE, GERMANY, started building the family fortune in 1838, with a small grocery store at Delmer and 6th Street in St. Louis. The light lager he introduced to the city was a great hit, and a brewery was built in 1840 near what is now the Gateway Arch. The limestone cave system at the corner of Cherokee and DeMenil Place, used for lagering the beer in icy refrigeration, helped Lemp's Western Brewing Company win first place amongst beers at the 1858 St. Louis World's Fair.

When Johann died, on August 25, 1862, he was a millionaire, and his son, William, would begin a major expansion of the brewery, purchasing five blocks on Cherokee, above the limestone ice-filled caves. In 1864, a new plant was built at Cherokee Street and Carondolet Avenue, covering five city blocks. By the 1870's, the Lemp family was riding high on the success of its product. Jacob Feickert, William Lemp's father-in-law, built a Victorian showcase home in 1868, the Lemp Mansion, near the Lemp brewery. The tunnel beneath the mansion, from the basement to the brewery, was only one very strange facet of the place.

"Was this really Great Uncle Charles' farm?" Betsy, the young Lemp niece, asked of her older brother Charles, also known as Charlie. She was sixteen and Charlie twenty as they gazed about at the wooded grounds of their great uncle's remote rural estate on this May afternoon in 1980, thirty-one years to the day since their great uncle had been buried here. Giant oak and elm trees towered above them. Flower gardens nearby wafted heady floral fragrances their way. All attention was focused on a man with a shovel in the foreground who was digging a hole. The family was loosely clustered around the gravedigger, as he attempted to locate the last known resting place of their Great Uncle Charles Lemp's ashes.

Young Charlie answered, "That's the weird part. Nobody really knows where Uncle Charles' farm *was*. We're out here today trying to find him... if he's even here. The family wants to transfer his earthly remains to the family crypts at Bellefontaine Cemetery, where all the rest of the Lemps are buried. I sure hope they find that wicker basket soon. It's getting hot out here, and I'm getting hungry." Young Charles took out a handkerchief and mopped his sweaty brow, before continuing. "Old Charles was a bit of an odd duck. He didn't do things quite like the rest of the family. Wasn't even ever in the beer business like the rest of them. He kicked around in that house like Howard Hughes or somebody for a long time. After he shot himself, Old Charles left explicit instructions that he be cremated and buried in a wicker basket on his estate. Wouldn't let the family post a death notice or wash his body or clean him up in any way, even if they wanted to. Weird. All the rest of the family is over at the Bellefontaine Cemetery. They feel it's time Old Charles joined the Lemp party.   But Charles, bless his eccentric little heart, wanted to be out here in a wicker basket on some godforsaken farm for eternity, buried like somebody's pet poodle. Let's just hope they find him. Fast. Otherwise, he's gonna' be pissed and I'M gonna' be pissed!" Charlie grinned his lopsided grin at Betsy. Betsy could never remain stern with Charlie when he smiled at her like that.

Betsy returned her brother's smile. She had not really known Great Uncle Charles at all. From what she did know, he was one odd duck. He was phobic about germs and wore rubber gloves all the time, for one thing.

"At least Great Uncle Charles had the good sense to leave a signed note before he committed suicide. None of the others left a note," said Betsy.

"What did the note say?" Charles IV did not know this gory detail.

"It said, 'In case I am found dead, blame it on no one but me,'" said Betsy.

"Well, duh," Charlie said. "Sounds like something one of the Three Stooges would say. Did he punctuate it correctly?

"What do you mean?"

"You know: put a comma after the word 'dead'?"

"Oh, Charlie!" Betsy hit him on the sleeve of his seersucker jacket with her white glove. "Just because you're a writer, you don't have to be so persnickety about punctuation. It was a suicide note, for crying out loud! He had a lot on his mind when he wrote it. In fact, it was dated the day *before* he killed himself, so he must have been thinking of killing himself for at least twenty-four hours."

Betsy continued. "Well, he was found dead, all right. Just like Will and Elsa and William. Four from the same family. You *did* know that four of our relatives killed themselves, right?"

Charles seemed shocked. "No! Four? What? When?"

"You see? That's what happens when you're just too busy living out East being a writer and a playboy. You lose sight of the important hereditary nature of our family's all-consuming desire to off themselves. Usually successfully." Betsy gave Charlie an arch look from beneath one cocked eyebrow.

Charles IV kicked at a clod of dirt as the sweating gravedigger continued his excavation, the shovel making a horrible noise as annoying as fingernails on a chalkboard. The assembled crowd all fervently hoped that the hired muscle would find the last resting place of Great Uncle Charles quickly.

"How did they all die?" Charlie was wide-eyed with interest. "I mean…I know that they killed themselves, but how?"

"Well, Great Uncle Charles here shot himself with a 38 Caliber Army Colt revolver. He was found in bed clutching the gun and, of course, he left the note. He had lived alone in that creepy old mansion at 3322 De-Menil Place, with just two servants, for years."

"It might be a creepy old mansion to you, Betsy, but it was a grand place in its day. They used to have an entire auditorium beneath the place that stretched under the street and allowed actual plays to be put on by traveling Chautauqua troupes. They rigged up sets and lights and the whole nine yards. And a swimming pool! That place had a swimming pool beneath it. Imagine! Your own private swimming pool with water heated by the brewery's boiler house. Wouldn't that be grand? To have your own private heated underground swimming pool way back in the 1860's?" Charlie, lost in contemplation, seemed cheered by the thought.

Betsy was less cheerful. She was sweating so profusely that her new white dress was being ruined. She continued, "There used to be a spiral staircase to get to all that stuff. It ran twenty-two feet down to the theater from the intersection of Cherokee and DeMenel, but they took it out and sealed it up, to prevent access. Mostly, Prohibition did the Lemps in."

"But," said Charlie, "people were killing themselves long before Prohibition made life tough for people who sold beer. Look at Frederick Lemp, William's son. He died when he was only twenty-eight, in 1901."

"Yes, he died young," said Betsy, "but at least he didn't shoot himself in the head like the rest of the family. He just died of heart failure. Overwork, they said. You do realize, big brother, that Frederick's death at such a young age left his father William totally devastated and was a contributing factor to his eventual suicide? William withdrew from the world. In fact, that tunnel system that you think would have been so much fun was William's way of getting to work from then on. Walked to work below ground. William just couldn't stand it when his son died. Frederick was the one who was supposed to take over the business, and then he up and died."

"Yes, but, at least he died of *natural* causes," said Charles IV.

"There's nothing natural about the way our relatives die off in droves. William finally offed himself on February 13, 1904, right after breakfast. Told the servants he didn't feel well, took a .38 caliber Smith & Wesson revolver, and shot himself in the head."

Young Charles mimicked a gun being put to his temple and the trigger being pulled. Betsy shook her head in disgust.

"That's just so sad, Charles. You shouldn't make fun. What a sad, sad family we have."

"You've got *that* right," said young Charlie. "William, Jr., didn't fare much better. He married the Lavender Lady."

"Who's the Lavender Lady?" Betsy really did not know as much as she was *pretending* to know about her family's past.

"Her name was Lillian Handlin. Bill, Jr., married her in 1899. From that point on, Bill and Lillian seemed to have a race to see which one of them could run through the family money the fastest! Lillian always wore lavender, so they called her 'the Lavender Lady.' She was quite the arm candy, but Bill couldn't take her spendthrift ways, so he divorced her a couple of years later, creating a huge scandal in the city gossip columns. People claim that they see the ghost of the Lavender Lady in the Lemp Mansion, you know."

"No, really?" Betsy seemed awed by this piece of information.

"Oh, yeah. The whole place is as haunted as hell! Doors lock themselves and then unlock themselves. There are cold places. People feel as though they're being watched. And then, of course, there were the rest of the deaths."

"What rest of the deaths?" Betsy parroted.

"You really don't know that much, do you?" Charles laughed at Betsy's apparent ignorance in the face of her know-it-all attitude as he said this.

"Well, Mother didn't think we should dwell on the bad stuff," answered Betsy. She sounded defensive.

Charlie began his lecture. "You know about Franklin, dead at twenty-eight, of, as you put it, 'natural causes.' Then his father, William, blew his brains out. Then there was Elsa."

"Aunt Elsa?"

"Who else?

"I always thought that Elsa's husband murdered her. That's what Mom said once."

Charlie shook his head up and down affirmatively. "Well, you do have a point, little girl. Some people did think that her March 20, 1920, death was a bit strange. She and the hubby had been having some marital difficulties. Then, they got back together. Shortly after that: BANG!" Betsy jumped as Charlie, once again, did the imaginary gun to temple thing and provided the appropriate sound effect.

"It's a good thing that the digging is over and we're far enough away from that basket hole so that nobody heard that, Charlie," laughed Betsy. "You really need to have more respect for the dead. And for the family."

"Oh, I have all the respect in the world for this bunch of loons. But, as for Mom's theory that Elsa was murdered, Mom does have a point. The loving husband didn't notify the authorities that Elsa had taken a bullet to the brain for two hours. Strange, don't you think?"

"What did he give as his reason for the delay?" Betsy was processing this information.

"The usual: I was upset. I wasn't thinking straight, blah, blah, blah."

"So, Aunt Elsa might have been murdered?"

"Well, the brothers didn't seem to think so. When Will and Edwin, her brothers, showed up at the house and were told that Elsa had shot herself in the head, Will just said, 'That's the Lemp family for you!'"

Charlie made a funny matter-of-fact Laurel & Hardy gesture, as though to say, "Another fine mess you've got me into." Betsy couldn't help but laugh, even though she was cross with Charles for making light of the family's long tragic history.

"So, then, let me see if I have this right. First, Frederick dies young. Then, his dad William shoots himself in the head. Then, Elsa. Who else? You said four. That's only two that actually committed suicide," Betsy crossed her arms across her chest, as though she had just won an argument.

"After the 1920 shooting of Elsa, which, as you have pointed out, Mom thinks may have been a murder of Elsa by her estranged husband, the next to bite the bullet was Will, Jr, on December 29, 1922, about two years after Elsa shuffled off this mortal coil." When Charlie used the term "bite the bullet," the pun was intentional, and he mimicked biting a bullet. "Will, Jr., talked to his wife on the phone from his office. Then, he shot himself in the heart with a .38 caliber revolver, right through his best shirt. And here's another gory detail for you. His funeral was held right in the Lemp Mansion, in his office, on December 31, 1922, two days later. But Will is interred in the Bellefontaine Cemetery in the crypt right above his sister, Elsa. You might say that they have bunk beds there. As for wives, those Lemp boys sure knew how to pick 'em.'"

"Stop, Charlie! That's too grim!" As she said this, Betsy laughed in spite of herself. "So, after Will, Jr., only Great Uncle Charles, he of the wicker basket, counts as one of our esteemed ancestors who ate their gun?" In spite of herself, Betsy was amused. Charlie could always make her laugh.

"Yes. Don't you think that's enough? Frederick dies young. William, his father, shoots himself. Oh! And there was also the fact that William's best friend, Frederick Pabst, died on January 1, 1904, which was quite close to young Frederick's death. William was depressed by these two deaths, as you can imagine."

"Pabst? As in Pabst Blue Ribbon?" Betsy asked.

"Yeah. It seems that our ancestors were quite helpful to other brewers, allowing them to get started in the beer biz, that is. Then, of course, our Lemp luminaries sold the name 'Falstaff' and the logo to Joseph Grisedieck for $25,000. Here's a shrewd business move for you," Charlie said sarcastically, in a hushed tone. "The brewery was worth $7 million before Prohibition. Guess how much Will sold it for in 1911?"

"I dunno," Betsy said, "Three million?"

"Not even close, Betsy Baby. $588,000. But Will's mom had died of cancer in 1906. She was sick with it since 1905, and Will was just not playing with a full deck at that point in time. If you ask me, this family didn't need beer; it needed Lithium or one of those other bi-polar drugs. AND a good attorney! And then, of course, Prohibition came, and the Depression. The times sure didn't help. But these family geniuses sold the brewery to the International Shoe Company for about one-fourteenth of its real value." Charles almost sounded like he was going to start making the old-fashioned "tsk tsk" noise.

"So…did anybody in this family ever die of natural causes? Besides Frederick, I mean?" Betsy asked this with a look that was both hopeful and horror-struck.

"Well, there was Edwin. He died in 1970 at age ninety of natural causes. But he insisted that all his paintings and all papers related to the family be burned when he died. Terrible thing. There was irreplaceable historical value to some of those documents." Charlie sighed and shook his head.

"Who owns the Lemp Mansion now, Charlie?"

"Guy named Paul Pointer. It was a boarding house for a while, but he runs it as a restaurant/bar/hotel. It's spooky as hell in there, too. In the seventies, they renovated it, and half the workers left the job because of all the weird shit that went down while they were working. Noises. Tools disappearing. Just strange stuff."

Charles, seeing that an ancient soiled wicker basket was finally in possession of the gravedigger, took Betsy's elbow to escort her back to their car. "If you go there for dinner or stay overnight, you're likely to hear ghostly knocks, phantom footsteps. Hell! The glasses in the bar have been known to fly right off the bar with nobody near 'em. The piano in the bar plays by itself. And it's NOT a player piano. Did you see last month's issue of *Life* magazine?"

"No, why?" asked Betsy.

"You should really try to keep up, Betsy. The Lemp Mansion was named one of the ten most haunted places in the United States by *Life* magazine. That's our family's legacy."

"Really?" Betsy asked.

"Really," said Charlie.

"No wonder Mom would never let me visit the place, "said Betsy. "I don't even know where it is."

"You take Broadway from Interstate 55 and follow that to Cherokee Street. Go west on Cherokee and turn right onto DeMenil Place. Address is 3322 DeMenil Place. Wanna' go have dinner there right now?"

Betsy shot him a furtive glance and said, "No, thanks. Maybe another time."

Charlie just laughed as they slid across the leather seats of his Buick convertible.

"Okay. No Lemp Mansion food, then. Let's go find some of those St. Louis ribs that I'm always hearing about back East."

Charles Lemp, IV, started the car and Charles and Betsy drove slowly down the tree-lined lane, their attention turning from death to life.

Queen Bee

ANGER: **"I WOULD LIKE TO SMACK** Linda Donaldson right up alongside her head. Just smack her a good one! Everyone has to kow-tow to her…the Queen Bee. Barking orders like a drill sergeant! She isn't even subtle about it any more. It's just 'Do this!' or 'Do that!'"

Helen Nelson was complaining…again… to her long-suffering husband, Larry, who was…again…not listening.

Helen went on, "Her Christmas card last year featured a picture of the Lutheran Church. The Lutheran Church isn't even *her* church! She's a Methodist! She just selected some random church! I was coerced into buying chance after chance on baskets of crap for her pet Methodist church projects. 'Hey, Linda! I have a church, too! You wanna' contribute to *my* church's collection basket?' No? …Somehow, I didn't think so."

Helen was just warming to her topic, talking to Larry, who, as usual, was ignoring her.

"Every month, she makes that poor pussy-whipped husband of hers do something for 'the church.' Paint this. Sell tickets to that. Help with this. Ice cream social that. Make the sets for that puppet show. Wipe my shoes while I take over all control of the play from the director. Kiss my ass! Poor guy. I'd feel sorry for him, except that he's at least fifteen years older than she is. He should know better," said Helen as she folded the dishtowel and replaced it on the oven door handle. "You'd think he would just tell her to go get fucked. But, noooooooooooo! Not the Queen Bee! We ALL must do the Queen Bee's bidding! Besides," and Helen smiled at this, "who would do the fucking? Certainly not him!"

IDEA: "Queen bee. Hmmmmmm. Wouldn't it be GREAT if a bee really stung her on her fat ass? Especially since she's allergic and all. Nothing like a little anaphylactic shock to put that woman right! That, or a good screwing, which is probably what she's needed for years. But since her husband sleeps with one of those godawful sleep apnea contraptions on his face, somehow I doubt that there is much screwing going on at 110 East Oak Street. I wonder if David Donaldson ever tried to pick up chicks with that octopus-like thing on his face." Helen chuckled at the thought. Then she murmured, "Bees. Hmmmm."

SEGUE: Helen Nelson drove to the edge of Pottsville, where the Drurys lived. John Drury was a bee-keeper. He emerged from the nearby fields with the hat and netting still draped over his head and greeted her from beneath the explorer-like hat.

"Hi, Helen!" he half yelled, half mumbled from beneath this ridiculous get-up.

"What can I do for you this morning?"

EXCUSE: "Well, John…I don't know much about bee-keeping, but I'd like to learn. Do you think you could give me a crash course in bee keeping? I know that you have enjoyed it as a hobby, for years. Larry mentioned that he would like to learn how to make our own honey. We have that extra field out back. Besides, if we started making our own honey, we could have business cards made up with something catchy…something like, 'Sweet City.' Then, I could use the business cards to get in to the wholesale jewelry show in Vegas later this month. It's just a couple weeks away. All you need is a Tax-payer ID number or a business card, my friend Shirley says. 'Sweet City' business cards would do the trick. And there's that new holiday, 'Sweetest Day.' Gifts of honey could be good for that occasion, too." Helen smiled at John. Sweetly.

She was surprised at how easily this lie came to her. This wasn't going to be hard at all!

INTRIGUE: When the hives were all set up in a row on the small field behind their house, Helen covered herself with the netting and the veil and reached in to find the biggest, meanest bee of the bunch. She was pretty sure she had found her…a Queen Bee that would certainly do damage to other Queen Bees.

It was 9:30 a.m. on Sunday morning. Church would be starting at the Methodist Church at 10:00 a.m. It was spring. The church windows were always open in the spring, to let the air circulate. Gee…it would be too bad if a bee flew through that open church window and stung Linda Donaldson. Wouldn't it? What a tragedy that would be!

POST MORTEM: The coroner diagnosed Mrs. Donaldson's death as a case of sudden and acute respiratory distress, caused by the swelling of the airways following a bee sting. Severe anaphylactic shock. What a shame! Linda Donaldson never knew what hit her! Or, in this case, what stung her.

But the choir certainly sounded lovely…up until the commotion broke out.

And the jewelry Helen Nelson was wearing at the funeral was absolutely gorgeous! Such a good deal, too! It was, well, sweet.

Helen Nelson smiled inwardly as she admired the sunlight glinting in rainbow-like colors off her new three-carat diamond ring. 'Sweet City,' indeed.

Circle Five: the Wrathful

A WRATHFUL FATHER IN THE PARK...
Welcome to the fifth circle of hell!

The Ghost Girl of
Howard "Pappy" Litch Park

IT IS JUNE, 2003, IN GALENA, KANSAS, and the Galena Good Old Days celebration is in full swing in the newly dedicated Howard "Pappy" Litch Park. The park is named for Howard "Pappy" Litch, a local historian and beloved citizen of Galena, Kansas. The land for Litch Park was once a federal weighing station, but Darrell Ray of Joplin, Missouri, worked tirelessly to establish a memorial to the Will Rogers Highway, (also known as Route 66), on this very land.

"I think that we should try to preserve as much of the spirit of the good old days of Route 66 as we can," Darrell said in a newspaper interview documenting the many monuments he had helped establish up and down Route 66. Mr. Ray spent his life on projects devoted to memorializing the highway popularized in both the television series of the same name and the Bobby Troup song. In a sad foreshadowing of what would happen during Galena's June, 2003, *Good Old Days* celebration, Darrel Ray died of a heart attack the Thursday before he was supposed to be present in Litch Park at the celebration of the Mother Road.

The celebration went on without Darrell Ray, or, for that matter, without Howard "Pappy" Litch, who had been dead for years when the park was named after him. Galena residents flocked to the site to dedicate the green, grassy area. What was happening at Litch Park this day was lots of music. Various bands had set up on stages in the park. Street musicians like Kenny Keene were welcome, too, and Kenny had brought his slide guitar to entertain the crowd.

Three children—Hannah, Emma and Jack—sit wordlessly on the grass in Litch Park, entranced by the music. It's their divorced Dad's day to entertain his three children. The oldest child, Hannah, a girl of eight clad in pink shorts, plays with her pigtails. The pigtails have matching pink bows, pretty against Hannah's flaxen hair and angelic face. Hannah's sister, Emma, two years younger, is wide-eyed and quiet, awed by the music and the crowd and the trees above. The littlest child, their younger brother Jack, diaper-clad, sucks on a pacifier, waving a toy tractor like a dangerous gunslinger, as though, at any moment, he might gouge out his own eye or that of one of his sisters. Jack wears a floppy sun hat that makes him appear absurd. At the very least, he is a concussion waiting to happen. Little Jack stomps his right foot on each downbeat as the slide guitar man plays louder and the music grows more frantic.

"Jack, sit down!" Hannah commands the boy as though she is his mother.

"Ooog!" From Jack, this is high praise. Jack has not yet begun to speak in sentences, and, with his penchant for sucking on a pacifier, he might not say anything intelligible at all for a few years.

The brown-hatted street performer, intent, concentrates on the intricate fingerwork, his mouth working in a weird warped way.

The musician says, "I wrote this next one at a kitchen table in Independence, Kansas," and sings, "The sky above me brings me down..."

The weather in the new Howard "Pappy" Litch Park is beautiful, balmy and eighty-four degrees. The musician delivers the refrain perched on a bar stool in the shade of a canopy of "Y"-shaped grasshopper-green trees on this brilliant spring day. A battery atop a large wagon powers the microphone that carries his original melodies to two hundred attentive listeners arrayed in a ragged semi-circle. He is a street musician, and a good one.

The father seats his brood of three in a row down front.

"Hannah, take Emma's arm. Jack, come back here." Dad is having trouble corralling the active boy, but once Hannah, the eldest, sits down, Emma and Jack also sink to the grass. Jack is already on his feet again, stomping his right foot along with the bass-line of the song.

"Why do I have to sit next to Jack?" Emma asks. She knows the answer. Nobody will really be sitting next to Jack. Jack will be on his feet most of the time in that always-on-the-go way little kids have.

Obedient, good kids, they follow their older sister's lead in seating themselves, although Emma pouts when Dad ignores her pleas to be placed further from young Jack. Emma tries to distance herself from Jack and Hannah throughout the day, and that helps some to explain what happens later.

The silver metallic slide guitar the man is playing enthralls Hannah, especially the way his fingers caress the strings, flying across them. She stares intently at the man's rapid-fire fingers, as he works the frets nimbly, seated only ten feet in front of them, his right sandal-clad foot tapping out the beat on a piece of wood.

Aligned in a row in yoga lotus position, the trio of children watch the musician manipulate the slide guitar. They look as though, if they could understand this, it might reveal some secret of life. They are mesmerized. A smattering of crowd applause greets each new riff, the next run faster than the last. The music reverberates, crescendoes.

"Thank you, ladies and gentlemen. And kids, " the singer says, nodding and smiling towards his front-row audience of three. "Anything you can donate today is appreciated. CD's are for sale to the left. Just ask the lovely Misty, who's over there holding them up. She'll be happy to sign them for you." The blue bucket rapidly fills with green bills; the tempo of the musical selections increases.

"Daddy, can we buy a CD?" Hannah asks. The line forming in front of the blonde sandal-clad Misty is long. People are hungry to take home a moment of musical magic. The black-clad father stands near his seated children, plastic beer cup in hand.

"We'll see." The generic parental non-answer for the ages.

Dad is a nondescript man of perhaps forty, six feet tall, clad in black tee shirt and black jeans. He has the athletic look of a man who once played football. A protective papa, he reaches down to adjust the goofy hat his young son wears, shielding the boy from the sun's rays. He tousles Emma's hair, and she giggles.

"You like the guitar man, Kids?" he asks, between songs.

"Yes, Daddy. Can we get his CD? Can we?" Hannah is fanning the flames of consumerism on this glorious day. Soon the others will join in, trying to wear their father down.

Glancing down at the fascinated kids as they follow every riff from the accomplished musician in the battered brown hat, Dad smiles a father's proud smile, beer cup in hand.

A young couple approaches, assuming a position directly in front of the children. The young girl of the duo is perhaps eighteen, wearing hoop earrings and a gray poncho. She leans her head against the young man's shoulder. Her boyfriend wears flannel pajamas in a wild blue plaid print. A white tee shirt completes his outfit. He looks warm, sweaty and uncomfortable as he plays with the girl's left earring, which is as big around as her wrist. The boy's arm below the tee shirt's cuff bears a barbed wire tattoo. The couple is oblivious to everyone, indifferent to all stimuli but the music and their bodies, pressed together so closely that they look as though they could melt into a giant blob under the sun's rays. Together, merged in a romantic tableau, the teenagers form an impenetrable barrier, obscuring the view of all those behind them in the crowd, especially the view of the three small seated children. The young couple's wishes and desires are all that matter to them. Their view, their entertainment, their experience is paramount. Only the hypnotic beat of the singer's music interests them, and the pressure of flesh on hip, girlfriend against boyfriend, bodies leaning against each other, confirming their union, melding two into one.

The father realizes that his children no longer can see the performer. He steps forward and lightly taps the young man on his right shoulder. Nothing. A second polite tap. Pajama boy pays no attention to the older man.

The father steps closer to the young man's right shoulder a third time and whispers in his ear.

"Young man, could you and your date move just a few feet to the side, so that my kids can see the guitar player?" The father smiles as he asks the question. The young man gives no sign he has heard, not even glancing at the older man. The young couple remain stationary.

The father stands there, fuming. No words are necessary to convey his anger, his frustration. His emotions are transparent, a silent movie, no sub-titles necessary. An incident is about to play out. A dark look bruises the father's furious eyes. His agitated state grows with every passing second. His body tenses like a cat preparing to spring. In a frantic burst of energy, the older man moves two to three feet ahead of the couple and places his body directly in front of the impassive pair. He turns and says to the indifferent duo behind him, "How do you like it?"

The couple doesn't respond or react.

The father stands there, almost quivering with rage. He tries to block the couple's view as they have blocked his children's gaze, but he is only one man.

Jack no longer waves his small toy tractor in time to the music. His foot no longer stomps along with the bass-line. He no longer smiles. The children's concentration is fragmented. The oldest girl, Hannah, now wears a look of growing concern. Their mood of happy enjoyment is shattered.

The black-clad father abruptly returns to his place behind the couple, four feet in back of them, standing next to his three children. He leans forward again, towards the young man's right shoulder, takes one step forward, and says, into the pajama-clad boy's right ear, "Screw you!"

The boy turns, slowly, looks at the unhappy man. "What did you say?"

"I said 'Screw you, you low-life. These are little kids here. They were here first. You're ruining their good time."

The children remain seated on the ground. They now look as though they might spring to their feet and take flight. Hannah, the oldest girl, has begun twisting the pink ties on her pigtails faster, a gesture of worry. She squints up at the overarching lattice-like canopy of trees above their heads. Emma, clad in a pink and orange top and blue jeans, studies her sister's upturned face tensely from a distance, trying to decipher what has happened. Her glance flits from face to face like a darting moth. She distances herself a bit from her siblings, sitting three to four feet away. Little Jack begins to lose interest, starts to look away, and drops his toy tractor in the dirt. Jack will cry soon. It's evident in the way he stops dancing."

The teen-aged boy looks amused. "Well, excuuuuuuuuuse me," he says, in an imitation of an old "Saturday Night Live" skit line he has heard in countless re-runs. He turns his back, once again ignoring the older man.

Irate, the father thrusts his hands deep into his pocket. He is almost apoplectic with rage. He pulls his right hand from his jacket pocket, the fingers wrap around an object. Something metallic glitters on his palm, catches the sunlight. Glints there, but only can be seen briefly.

The song ends.

"We're gonna' take a little break to tune the guitars here, folks. We'll be back in a few. Thanks so much for your contributions. Any money helps keep us on the road. Please be considerate; throw us a buck. Be considerate of your fellow park people, too." The singer has noticed the developing trouble, and he has done what he can to help while hitting up the crowd for one last donation before taking a break. And, hopefully, before real trouble starts. A crowd engulfs the singer, gathering around him for autographs. The father still seethes with anger.

The young couple finally breaks their static pose. They move down the gravel of the park's pathway, towards the rose bushes, away from the father and his three cheated children. Slowly ambling, the lovers are in no hurry.

The older man reaches out to his restless children, helps them to their feet.

"Stay here just a minute, Honey," he says to Hannah, the oldest. "Watch Emma and Jack."

"But, Daddy…" Hannah starts to protest, but Dad is gone, following pajama-boy and his date deeper into the park. The metallic object is just barely visible, concealed inside his left hand. The pajama-clad boy is now within two feet of the frustrated parent.

At some point, the boy and his girlfriend nonchalantly cross directly in front of the man, rudely cutting him off. The lovers are strolling at a leisurely pace, unconcerned, oblivious, arms around each other's waists. The couple and the furious father approach a remote and heavily wooded area of the Howard "Pappy" Litch Park. Few of the day's celebrants are present in this area, as the bugs are out in force here.

The father opens his hand, takes the silver thing, places the brass knuckles over the fingers of his right fist.

"Hey! Punk! I'm not going to excuuuuuuse you." The older man swings hard and a bright burst of red sprays from the teen-aged boy's nose.

The girlfriend screams and jumps on the father's back. He responds by yanking at one of her giant earrings, pulling it from her ear. She collapses in the grass, sobbing.

"Maybe you won't be such a jerk next time we're celebrating the Good Old Days." The father stands above the younger man, seemingly triumphant; the boy seems shocked to have been attacked.

Others in the park are beginning to notice the brief, violent encounter. The angry father suddenly remembers that he must return to his three children. He turns to go, but pajama boy rises from the grass and launches himself at the older man's turned back in a counter-attack.

"Okay, you two. Break it up. Come with me." The policeman interposes himself between the two struggling male forms and escorts them to another part of the park, ignoring the father's pleas.

"I've gotta' get back to my kids, Officer. They're waiting for me."

"I see. And that's why you attacked this young man unprovoked?" The officer doesn't seem sympathetic; he had witnessed the first blow from across the park's green expanse, but not the lead-up to the fight.

"No…it wasn't unprovoked. But, right now, I've got to get back over there. Come with me. I'll explain later." Dad points to the general area where the performer, now gone, had been singing, and where his children had been sitting.

Eventually, the officer agrees to lead the man to the area where he says his kids are waiting for him. Hannah is there, holding little Jack on her lap.

"Where's Emma?" Dad asks.

Hannah looks up, terrified, red-eyed from crying. "I don't know, Daddy. She was here, but I was chasing Jack. And then she was just… gone."

Hannah whimpers a bit, all that is left of the active crying she has been engaged in for over half an hour. A crowd gathers around the two small children, comforting the crying girl and her brother.

The father shouts to the people around Hannah. "Did anyone here see a little girl, about six, wearing a pink and orange top, blonde hair and blue eyes? Answers to the name Emma?"

A murmur runs through the crowd, as though they are reluctant to speak. Finally, one woman comes to the front of the anxious group.

"I saw a woman come by and pick up a little girl dressed like that. I thought it was her mother." The stranger seems almost apologetic, as though she is somehow to blame for not questioning the woman about her actions at the time.

"How long ago? Which way did she go?" It is the Officer who is now asking questions. He is gradually accepting the father's concerns as his own.

"I don't know how long…maybe twenty minutes? She went towards the parking lot."

Everyone rushes to the parking lot. No sign of Emma.

Dad, distraught, hugs Hannah and Jack, comforting both of them. The young man looks on, surly, nursing his bloody nose, his girlfriend holding a Kleenex to her equally bloodied ear.

There was never any description of the kidnapper provided that could help the police locate the mystery woman who took little Emma during the Good Old Days celebration in Galena, Kansas. Some said the kidnapper was young and blonde. Some said she was tall and brunette. After taking testimony from the crowd, which had not realized that the woman was not Emma's mother, the descriptions were so varied as to be useless. No one saw the woman place the youngster in a vehicle. Some did say that Emma was crying, but Jack and Hannah were also crying, so Emma's tears did not seem out-of-the-ordinary. She was only six, after all.

Every year in the four years since the event, residents who visit Howard "Pappy" Litch Park in Galena, Kansas, report hearing a crying child when the park is deserted. They also sometimes see a small figure, clad in pink-and-orange, climbing on the playground equipment—the swings, the jungle gym—near dusk, but, when the observers draw near, no child is present. At night, the strains of slide guitar music seem to waft through the park, coming from far, far away, and, sometimes, the sound of children crying seems to accompany the sad music, like an echo.

Circle Six: Heretics

AN AMISH FATHER PAYS the ultimate price for allowing his daughter to stray from the path of righteousness…

A young girl is kidnapped and indoctrinated into a cult with deadly results…

Hell to Pay

"Nunc Lenta Sonita Dicunt Morieris"
"Now, this bell tolling softly for another, says to me: Thou must die."

When Jacob Yoder's cell phone rang loudly inside his pocket while he was at the sale barn selling his grain, the ring attracted immediate attention. "Do not ask for whom the bell tolls", wrote John Donne. "It tolls for thee". The cell phone bell, ringing softly in Jacob's pocket was a small catastrophe.

I thought the ringer was set to silent, Jacob winced, with supreme regret, as he dropped his straw hat while fumbling to shut off the phone. The cell phone was ringing, playing "Amazing Grace;" all the other Amish gathered at the sale barn stared at Jacob. Jacob was not as proficient with modern technology as he wished he were, which was understandable. That could be blamed on the fact that he was not supposed to be dealing with modern technology at all.

Although the Amish were masters at side-stepping regulations to obtain rides to town in cars from their neighbors or to use telephone land lines, they were always supposed to ask themselves, "What kind of person am I becoming? Does this help or hurt the Amish community?" They all used diesel-powered engines to power their wood shop equipment. They ran diesel generators to charge a bank of 12-volt batteries, a charge that was then sent through a converter. This created homegrown 110-volt "Amish electricity." But there were limits. Always, there were limits. Amish life was an authoritarian life.

Across the room, Moses Borntrager scowled at Jacob, who was still fumbling in his jacket pocket, trying to stop the ringing. Moses frowned. He approached Jacob, glaring.

"Jacob Yoder, does thee have a telephone on your person?"

There was no point in denying it. That would only add lying to the list of sins that Jacob would be committing as a member of Buchanan County, Iowa's Old Order Amish. He looked up from under a furrowed brow, weathered from plowing, planting and harvesting under the Iowa sun and muttered one word: "Yes."

Jacob knew that the twenty or thirty families that constituted his Amish district would hear about his cell phone from Moses Borntrager. They would definitely hear about it. After all, it was Moses who had told Bishop Smucker about Mary.

Mary was Jacob's only daughter. Jacob's wife, Rachel, died giving birth to Mary. Jacob raised the child from infancy, encouraging her to be independent and self-sufficient. This was a double-edged sword. While Jacob read to Mary every night from the Bible and from the 1,000 page *Martyr's Mirror*, which told of the persecution and public executions of Anabaptist martyrs in Switzerland, Germany and Holland in the 1700's, Mary was always brimming over with questions.

"But, Daddy, why didn't the people there just let the Anabaptists be? Why did they kill them for being who they were?"

"I don't know, darling. I don't know."

"I don't think it's right to stop a person from being who or what they are. It's not right to tell another human being how to live his life. It's not right to rule over people in private religious matters, either. It's not right to rule over them in any way, really. Only God can direct humans in the right ways of the Lord." Mary's sky-blue eyes and flaxen hair, coupled with her sincerity, gave an angelic quality to this prescient wisdom.

For a child of only thirteen, she made more sense than most adults. Old beyond her years, some called it. That tended to happen when a child lost her mother young.

It didn't surprise Jacob when his intelligent only daughter decided she must attend school in Independence. Mary was bright. Very bright. Jacob had never seen a child of either sex pick up so quickly on so many things. He was proud of Mary's mind. But the Bible says, "Pride goeth before a fall." Nothing was worse, to the Amish community, than to call attention to one's self in any way. Like many other cultures, it was not right to encourage a child to be proud. An attitude of humility was to be maintained, an attitude so important to the Amish that they even had a special name for it, "Gelassenheit."

For the Amish, it was also a sin to be too well educated. In the 1960's, a picture taken outside a one-room schoolhouse in Buchanan County, Iowa, flashed round the world: young Amish children running into the cornfields to hide. Small elementary school-aged children running away to avoid being forced to go to the public school. The state of Iowa was attempting to enforce its laws that all schools must be state-certified and have state-certified teachers. The Amish one-room schoolhouse did not have a state-certified teacher. The bad publicity from that one photo soon made it clear that the Amish were going to get a special exemption from the state. No politician in his right mind wanted this kind of bad press! Brutal attempts to corral small children and send them to the town school were not popular in the world. The authorities caved. The Iowa legislature passed a law exempting the Amish from the laws governing all other Iowa schoolchildren.

Bishop Smucker put it this way: "Our children do not need more than an eighth grade education for a life on the farm. Leave us to our ways."

But Mary wanted to go to Independence to the public school. She thirsted for knowledge. She still felt that it was wrong for the Swiss, Dutch, and Germans to tell the Anabaptists how to worship and how to live. She felt she deserved the right to live life her own way, just like the Anabaptists in Europe in the 17th century deserved that right.

"Please, Daddy. I love you, but I must go. God would not be pleased if I did not try to realize my potential. You've always told me that."

Secretly, Jacob agreed with her. God help him: he agreed with Mary, not with the church.

At age fifteen, Mary left for the city: Independence, the county seat. It was a town of 5,000 people, a good twenty per cent of them mentally ill inmates of the largest State Mental Hospital in Iowa. The mental hospital was located on the west edge of town, its turreted castle-like buildings ominous on the horizon. The town, located at the junction of Highways 150 and 218, frequently hosted day-trip tourists on buses who browsed in the quaint shops. On Main Street there was a burger joint with fabulous French fries: White's Café.

Mary got a job at White's Café, slinging hash and waiting tables. Her phone call to Jacob on Sunday was all excitement.

"I've got a job, Daddy! A real job! I'm going to be paid to cook and to wait on customers. And they're going to teach me to run the cash register, too, at White's Café. I'm so excited!" Jacob savored the happiness in Mary's voice. "But I miss you, Daddy. I miss you."

"I know, little girl, I miss you, too. But I am always here. I'll always be watching over you. There'd be hell to pay if anyone tried to hurt you!"

Jacob's intensity made the statement sound sterner than he had intended. They both chuckled.

Mary saved all the money she earned to go to Iowa State University in Ames. She finished high school in three years, energized by her enthusiasm for learning all she could about everything. She was good at chemistry, biology, biochemistry, engineering. Because her father had raised her much like a son, Mary could fix anything on the farm, cook dinner, and, still clad in her prayer bonnet and with straight pins fastening the bodice of her plain blue blouse, she could fire up the old wood-burning stove and cook a fine meal. Some called the Amish "Hook-and-Eye Dutch" because they refused to wear buttons. Buttons reminded the Amish of their forced conscription into the military in the Old Country, which caused them to flee to America. Buttons meant military uniforms. Therefore, hooks-and-eyes were often used to close clothing. But Mary didn't have a mother to teach her to sew. She did what many of the Amish women did: used straight pins to hold her blouse closed. Jacob's face glowed with unspoken pride whenever Mary was near.

When word got out that Mary had left home for the public high school, it created a scandal amongst the Amish. The Bishop came to speak with Jacob. Jacob's dog, Sheila, a black lab he used for hunting, frolicked around Jacob's feet, unaware of the gravity of the stranger's mission.

"Jacob, Moses Borntrager told me of your Mary's rebellion. Thee must shun Mary. From now on she must be as though dead to you and to us. She has defied our ways. What kind of person is she becoming now, out amongst the English?" The Bishop looked quite appalled. His fleshy pig-like face flushed an unhealthy pink color. Spittle frothed at the corners of his porcine mouth.

Jacob stared intently at the floor of his farm great room. It was a plain room containing a wooden floor weary with age. The long Shaker table sat in the center, eight straight back chairs around it. Dark curtains, rather than real doors, were used to shield sleeping adults from the main room, in sleeping cubicles that were no more than six feet by eight feet. A large black iron stove, huge and hot, sat in the corner of the room, looming like a black widow spider. The day that the Bishop came, bread was baking. The yeast-y fragrance filled the room. In the August heat, with the tremendous heat thrown off by the old-fashioned wood-burning stove in the small room, beads of sweat rolled down Jacob's cheeks and lodged in his long brown beard. Jacob said nothing in response to the Bishop.

But Jacob remembered that Moses Borntrager had informed the Bishop. "Nunc Lenta Sonitu Dicunt Morieris."

Jacob could not give up his Mary. Never. He felt his heart shattering like broken glass in his chest. That was when Jacob bought the cell phone.

A cell phone dealer in town sold it to him. It was difficult to purchase, because Jacob, like all Amish, only paid cash.

John Walters, as Jacob approached his cell phone store, at first thought there must be some mistake.

"Can I help you?" he asked, politely.

"I want to buy a cell phone."

"Well," said John, cheerfully, "you've come to the right place!"

The two entered the low-slung one-story gray building on the outskirts of town. Jacob pulled up a hard wooden chair across from John's.

"We do a fair amount of sales here, but not so many of your people come in. Normally, we ask for a driver's license to activate the account. I know you don't have a driver's license. Maybe you have another form of identification?"

Jacob shuffled his feet. He had no other form of identification. The Amish didn't believe in photography. A driver's license was out of the question, even one that was simply a picture ID. Having one's picture taken was verboten, forbidden.

Jacob appeared perplexed…stymied.

John knew a little about the ways of the Amish. He knew that, for the Amish, having a cell phone was controversial and something that was being debated. He had been selling cellular systems for twelve years now, yet never had a member of the rural Amish community come to him. In Iowa City, his company had sold cell phones to the Mennonite Community of Little Amana, but that practice had not spread to the smaller towns yet. And, of course, Mennonite and Amish were different, despite the general public's perception that they were identical. Sales were slow, though, and he saw a way around Jacob's dilemma.

"Jacob, go get an Iowa state ID without a photograph, and then I can activate this account, if it's OK with your people."

"My bishop said that I could buy one for my farm foreman to use," lied Jacob.

Jacob got an ID, without a photo. What he really wanted, most of all, was some way to communicate with his beloved Mary. A cell phone was the perfect solution.

Jacob spoke with Mary daily throughout her three years in high school. She lived in Independence with a good Christian family who spoke with Jacob about Mary's choice. They treated her like a member of the family and Jacob paid them cash to feed, house and clothe her. Jacob was very proud of Mary's accomplishments. This, he knew, was also a sin against the Order. Mary completed high school early, first in her class. Her picture was in the newspaper. Another rule broken. The Order would frown on the publicity. Mary graduated and went on to Iowa State University in Ames on a full scholarship.

After he purchased the cell phone, Jacob tried to decide where to leave it.

Should I leave it in a shanty near the house? Should I leave it in the outhouse? Jacob smiled at the thought of sitting in the outhouse for hours, talking on the phone. *Should I leave the phone with an English neighbor?* English was what the Amish called the rest of the world, the outsiders. But then, how would Jacob keep it charged? No, Jacob must keep the phone hidden in the house. Because he did not want anyone to know that he was still communicating with his daughter. Jacob kept the cell phone hidden, another deep, dark secret.

But now, at the sale barn, with that secret revealed, other secrets would follow.

The ringing of the cell phone at the sale barn on Saturday morning alerted Moses Borntrager to Jacob's sin. The horses and buggies waited nearby, the horses' ears jerking spasmodically to protect against the omnipresent flies. The brown mares were covered with sweat and tethered to a hitching post. Jacob's Labrador retriever, Sheila, lay there quietly, head on paws, sleeping near the tethered horses.

"Jacob," Moses said, advancing at an angry pace on the flustered farmer, "having a cell phone is verboten! You cannot do this! Thou shalt not!"

"Why?" countered Jacob, his eyes flashing with momentary fire. "Isn't the Order all about the good of the group? About community? Does this new device bring us together or draw us apart? It seems to me that it brings us together. Therefore, it cannot be bad."

"Yes," admitted Moses, "a cell phone or a telephone can help us to communicate, but it must be used communally, like the old telephone rules. Thee must submit to the judgment of your peers. The question is:

what kind of person are you becoming as a result of using this blasphemous instrument? What will it lead to? It's not just the technology. It's how you use the technology. For what purpose? We will see what the Bishop has to say at the next District meeting in six months' time!" Moses harrumphed off to the far corner of the sale barn, casting a disapproving look backwards over his scandalized shoulder.

Jacob knew in his heart what the Bishop would say, in six months' time. Bishop Smucker was Old School. Extremely conservative. He thought back to that horrible hot August day when the Bishop came to him, like God came to Abraham in the Bible, telling him to give up his only child. He would not do it then. He would not do it now. What Jacob was about to do would be a mortal sin.

Since Jacob had nothing else to do in the evening, with Mary gone, he had been reading Mary's books on all the subjects she loved: biology, chemistry, biochemistry, engineering. He learned the subjects as she learned them.

"Mary, dear, what are you working on in your classes at the University now?" Jacob was making his weekly Sunday cell phone call to Mary's dorm room.

"Daddy, it's all just so fascinating! We're learning about viruses now. About how to engineer their DNA. Did you know that, if you alter the DNA of a virus just slightly, the virus could be adapted to a variety of uses?

Jacob was intrigued. "No, Mary. I did not know this. What kind of uses, Mary?"

"Well, the field I'm most interested in is called biomimicry. Using biomimicry, viruses can be altered to allow microbes to produce tiny transistor components, for example. Common harmless miniature factories can be made out of the viruses. They can produce semiconducting nano-particles. The nanoparticles then produce bio-sensors...things like liquid crystal structures for computers or memory chips."

Mary's voice was so excited that it made Jacob smile in empathy at her enthusiasm.

"That all sounds pretty complex for a simple farmer like me to understand."

"Oh, Daddy! You're every bit as smart as me. After all, where do you think I got my mental ability?" Mary scoffed.

"From your sainted mother Rachel, God rest her soul, of course," said Jacob. "But tell me more. I'm interested in learning everything you are learning, as you learn it."

"Well, Daddy, since these are organic structures, the lab equipment isn't that complicated. It's mainly the raw materials of viruses, microscopes, really nothing that elaborate."

Mary proceeded to describe the lab where she worked in great detail as her father listened intently.

"Oh! And Daddy! On Tuesday we had a guest lecturer in my Biochemistry class, one of the leading authorities in the field of viruses, Dr. E. Fuller. He was so interesting! His story is so sad, though. It made me think of all the poor patients at our Mental Health Institute. His theories might help them one day."

"What do you mean, Mary?" asked Jacob.

"Dr. Fuller's sister, Ellen, became schizophrenic. She was fine one day. The next day, she was outside their house in the snow telling people that she was Mary Magdalene. Completely out of her mind. She had to be institutionalized. She doesn't even recognize Dr. Fuller any more or any of the family. She doesn't speak. She's catatonic. It's just so sad. I know that, if you needed help, I would do everything in my power to try to help you, Daddy, and Dr. Fuller wants to try to help his poor sister."

"And I you, little girl. What is Dr. Fuller's plan for his sister?"

"Dr. Fuller has some pretty promising research going on. He has been fortunate enough to find a sponsor for his work, and he has some interesting theories about the origins of schizophrenia in humans."

"Really?"

"Dr. Fuller thinks that cats may cause schizophrenia in humans?"

"Cats?" Jacob's eyes widened in surprise, had Mary been able to see them.

"You know how women are told not to go near cats while they are pregnant?"

"Yes. I told your mother this, when she was carrying you."

"Well, Dr. Fuller isn't sure how the disease is triggered, but he found that Toxoplasma gondii, which can cross the placenta and harms the developing fetus in a pregnant woman, and causes deafness, seizures, mental retardation and cerebral palsy in the child, responded, in a petri dish, to antipsychotic medications and mood stabilizers. The drugs actually stopped T. Gondii in its tracks! Dr. Fuller also discovered that there are high levels of Toxoplasma antibodies in the blood of schizophrenics. Add to that this fact: when cats quit being regarded as pawns of the devil and began to be included in regular society as pets in the second half of the twentieth century, the incidence of schizophrenia sky-rocketed. Within twenty years in England and the United States, the admission to psychiatric hospitals tripled. Dr. Fuller isn't sure what the 'trigger' mechanism is that sets off the disease in people, but he thinks it may be exposure to cats. His theory is that it is an infectious disease like measles or the flu, caused by a virus."

"That is truly interesting, honey. How exactly does Dr. Fuller test his theories?"

Mary continued, explaining the lab set-up and the materials Dr. Fuller used.

"Oh! And Daddy…He doesn't just think that cats cause schizophrenia. He also has a theory that dogs may cause multiple sclerosis in humans."

"My goodness. This Dr. Fuller sounds like a very smart man, indeed. He's certainly full of interesting ideas for research. I hope you apply yourself to learn all you can from him, as I know you will."

"Yes, Daddy. I will do my best. I would like to work in this field, in the future, to help mankind."

"That's my girl!" Jacob beamed with pride.

After he hung up, Jacob pondered the good Doctor Fuller's theories, postulated in his quest to aid his schizophrenic sister. Soon, Jacob set up a lab in a corner of his workshop, just as Mary had described the one in which she worked daily at the university.

Dr. Fuller was not sure what the trigger mechanism for schizophrenia might be. His theory was that it was something in exposure to the droplets of cat feces that then lay dormant in the brain of the victim for years. Then, something unknown triggered the disease, just like the as-yet-unknown trigger for Type II diabetes in adults. Jacob pondered this problem for some time before he came up with an idea.

What if the trigger was not within man, but something present just in certain cats, instead? Within a matter of weeks, Jacob had isolated an enzyme in specific cats that he thought might be the culprit in triggering schizophrenia.

Jacob knew where to find the perfect test subject to test his theory. He only needed to secure a common housecat. The housecat that belonged to Moses Borntrager would do. Jacob injected the Borntragers' tabby with the viral trigger. Then, he sat back to watch. "Revenge is mine, saith the Lord" no longer had meaning for Jacob. Jacob had decided that Moses Borntrager would pay for driving a wedge between Jacob and his only child. *I can do some good for mankind while taking man's vengeance*, he thought. *There will be hell to pay for this loss of my daughter.* The bell was tolling for Moses and the Bishop. "Now, this bell tolling softly for another, says to me: Thou must die."

When the seizures first began, Moses Borntrager was petting his favorite barnyard cat, Lucy. Lucy had gone missing for a few days, so Moses was especially glad to see that she had come home. He petted the tabby cat for at least ten minutes in the barnyard, while the guinea fowl chased each other about, squawking noisily. Shortly afterwards, Moses fell to the ground, foaming at the mouth. He began shouting wildly.

"I am the risen Christ. He that believeth in me shall be saved. Mine is the kingdom of glory." This was followed by glossolalia, speaking in tongues.

The Borntrager family came running from the nearby pig-pens where they were slopping the hogs. Soon, Moses was in a room at the gothic Independence Mental Health Institute. Soon after that, he was blind. Soon after that, he was dead.

The Bishop was speaking from the pulpit when he first displayed symptoms. His eyes rolled back in his head. He fainted, falling backwards and hitting his head on the lectern. Blood from the head wound rained on the people nearby, like holy water on the congregation of a Catholic church. When the Bishop regained consciousness, he began screaming and hallucinating.

"Snakes! I see snakes! Don't you see them? They're everywhere! Look at the baseboard! Look at the floor. Snakes! Snakes! Pink snakes!" It took seven men to subdue him. It took eight men to get him into the straitjacket they brought from the Mental Health Institute. Ironically, the hysterical worshippers asked Jacob if they could borrow his cell phone to call the ambulance. Jacob smiled inwardly as he complied. The calico cat, the mouser for the Bishop's church, strolled across the altar nonchalantly as everyone worked feverishly to revive Bishop Smucker. Tabby looked unconcerned.

The Bishop was also taken to IMH. He lived one month before a particularly gruesome death. Left unattended momentarily, he jumped from the top parapet of the Gothic building, landing on the circular driveway, his rotund body making the sound of a smashed over-ripe pumpkin upon impact. Just before he jumped, Bishop Smucker screamed, "I'm coming to Jesus! I'm coming to Jesus! Beware the infidels!"

One-by-one, Jacob was evening the score. "Nunc Lenta Sonitu Dicunt Morieris."

Every day now, Jacob tinkered in his makeshift lab, working on new virus applications, trying to duplicate Mary's lab results.

Another theory existed regarding viruses that were animal-borne. This theory held that a virus carried by dogs caused multiple sclerosis in people. Jacob patted Sheila on her sleek black Lab head as he read the literature and tinkered in his secret laboratory.

Jacob's first symptom was a tingling in his legs. Then, his left hand began to cramp numbly. Things progressed rapidly. His muscles became completely uncompliant. They would not carry him nor do his bidding. By the time Mary was called to come for her father, Jacob was wheelchair-bound. He had lost the power of speech. His reflexes were poor. He trembled. He needed constant care. The doctors at the University of Iowa Hospitals and Clinics diagnosed multiple sclerosis, a disease not yet fully understood.

"Maybe some day," they told Mary, "there will be a cure. For now, all you can do is take him home and make him comfortable."

It was January. A bitter blizzard-like wind bit at Mary's fingers as she helped her father into her car. She struggled, alone, folding the heavy wheelchair to place in the trunk. It had snowed last night. Two feet of new snow made the highway slick and treacherous. She counted twenty-two cars in the ditch on her way from Ames to Iowa City in the sub-zero cold.

Mary felt helpless. All she could do was to try to comfort her father. He looked so old and frail and feeble. His head slumped against the window as he rested. He fell asleep almost immediately.

One thing that had always soothed Jacob was music, especially if Mary were singing.

Distraught at her father's debilitated condition, stricken with grief, Mary began softly humming his favorite hymn. Soon, she reached these stanzas in "Amazing Grace:"

"Yea, when this flesh and heart shall fail,
And mortal life shall cease,
I shall possess, within the veil,
A life of joy and peace.
The earth shall soon dissolve like snow,
The sun forbear to shine;
But God, Who called me here below,
Will be forever mine."

As Mary drove, glancing over at Jacob with concern, she saw a loving father who appeared to be sleeping. It was not until they reached Ames that Mary realized God had already called Jacob.

Now, God—and Mary—were forever his.

On Eagles' Wings

PSYCHIATRIC REPORT #1: NOVEMBER 3, 2005, DR. FIONA HIGGINS:
Ten-year-old Caucasian female discovered seated on the grass outside re-
mote Tualatin, Oregon cabin. Subject was rocking and humming to herself
when discovered. Family in cabin (Mother, Father, eight-year-old brother)
dead for about ten hours. Child unresponsive to questioning. Seems to be
in shock. Police are tracing car license plates to determine identity of the
victims.

Two hours later the police realized, after tracing the car's plates, that
this particular family was famous long before they died in a remote log
cabin in the woods near Tualatin, Oregon.

The Reynolds family: Gina and Thomas Reynolds, their ten-year-old
daughter, Adrienne, and her eight-year-old brother Phillip. This was the
young girl kidnapped by a bizarre cult and then returned to her family,
months later. Although sexually abused while a captive, she seemed to be
in good condition when rescued. A police officer had recognized her on
the streets of Tualatin. Soon, TV news shows were doing specials on her
return.

"What was it like in the hills, Adrienne? Were you frightened? Were
you tortured?" Diane Bennett of network TV. Diane gave Adrienne her
best pseudo-concerned intense gaze. Diane's blonde hair was perfectly
coiffed. She was about as smart as the ubiquitous birds.

After her return, Adrienne's flute lessons resumed. Weekly visits to a
psychiatrist began. Adrienne seemed to be doing well, despite the docu-
mented evidence of sexual abuse. The family thought that a week in the
rural, remote family log cabin in Tualatin would insulate them from the
media frenzy. The Reynolds' family's fame faded.

Now, Adrienne's entire family had faded to black.

During the courtroom proceedings, a strange tale emerged. The leader of the Manson-like "family", Bernard Burkin, was High Priest of a weird cult.

"I am the Chosen One. All who believeth in me shall be saved." Bernard was as coherent as a dung beetle and just about as attractive. Deranged. Grungy. Unshaven. Semi-hysterical. Bernard insisted on defending himself. This virtually assured him of a very long prison sentence. Folks in Oregon did not tolerate kidnapping and sodomizing ten-year-old girls. Oregon folks didn't take to that at all.

"Sit down, Bernie. If you don't sit down and shut up, the judge'll make you watch the proceedings on closed-circuit TV." Bailiff Hank Miller laid a gentle hand on Bernie's shoulder.

Bernard sat down and commenced rocking to and fro in his chair, drawing pictures of birds.

Burkin's "other" wife, Lila, smiling wanly, did not shed much light on the bizarre world that saw the three of them foraging for food in garbage cans while wandering from Oregon town to Oregon town, the women dressed in Burka-like garments. Lila did not seem too bright.

"Bernard is The One. We must do Bernard's bidding."

"Right, Lila," Hank said.

Many times Adrienne had almost been rescued during her six months of captivity. No one could explain why she had not tried to escape.

Now, Adrienne wasn't talking at all. Aside from humming the hymn "On Eagles' Wings," she was nearly catatonic.

"I shall lift you up where eagles soar," screamed the ragged-looking Burkin. His manic tone hastened his departure for the TV room. Most of his statements made no sense. Those that did make sense involved bird imagery.

"God wants me to teach everyone to fly. I know the ways of the eagles. I command the skies. They will lift us up. We must follow the birds. We must!" Burkin was shrieking.

"Beware the birds. Their wrath is mighty!" Bernie was ushered out for his daily dose of thorazine.

"Come on, Thoreau," Hank, the bemused bailiff, led Bernie out the door, "Next stop: Walden Pond."

The shackled prisoner shuffled from the packed courtroom, head down, eyes glazed, orange jump-suit crumpled.

It got even weirder after a visit to the cult's site in the woods. Carved statues of eagles and hawks. Bird-shaped votive candles. Incense. Weird

Mayan-like altars. Books of hieroglyphs resting on stands near altars. The police cryptographers were unsuccessful in deciphering their meaning.

"This is like that Egyptian exhibit at the museum. Look at all the friggin' birds! What-the-hell IS this stuff?" Lieutenant James Wilson, the first officer on the scene, leafed through one of the Bible-like books that stood on three ornately-decorated stands around the base of the main Oregon altar. The altar itself was pyramid-shaped, reminiscent of Chichen Itza.

Birds in nests. Birds flying. Birds sitting on tree limbs. Everywhere, birds. Beady eyes. Sharp beaks. Angry talons. Some stuffed eagles, wings outstretched, flying into infinity.

"I feel like I'm in a bad version of that Hitchcock movie 'The Birds,'" said Wilson. "except that these three aren't doing any running." The stench of the bodies caused Wilson to cover his mouth with his hat. He didn't have a handkerchief or mask. Soon, Wilson bolted for the pine-fresh air of the woods.

"What happened? Why is Adrienne outside in her nightgown, safe? The rest of the family, all of them dead ducks?" The bird joke he had just made was unintentional; no one was listening, anyway.

He examined eight-year old Phillip Reynolds, a small blonde boy whose body had been found in the top bunk wearing Spiderman pajamas. Phillip looked very vulnerable. Very frail. Lieutenant Wilson shook his head.

Psychiatric Report #2: November 5, 2005: *Adrienne is in the outer office waiting room of Dr. Fiona Higgins' office dressed in a hospital gown. Adrienne is humming quietly. Dazed. Disoriented. The tune she hums, over and over, is "I will lift you up on eagles' wings." Rocking back and forth, she occasionally curls into a fetal position.*

Following is the text of the conversation with Adrienne Reynolds three days after her discovery in Oregon:

Dr. Higgins: "Adrienne, can you hear me?"

No response.

"Adrienne, can you tell me what happened?"

"The birds didn't like it. The birds got mad."

"The birds got mad about what, Adrienne?" Dr. Higgins scribbles, pen busy on clipboard.

"The birds were mad and took them away."

"Took who away? How do you know that the birds were mad?" More notes. More furtive glances.

"They will lift us up on their wings." Quick glance from beneath Adrienne's long blonde lashes at Fiona. Eyes glazed. Rocking continuing.

"I fixed it. I made it better. Mr. Burkin said I had to. So I did."

Rocking, humming.

"Did what, Adrienne? How did you make it better? What did you do?" Fiona continues to make notations, glancing at the wan child before her. Fiona is a childless woman in her thirties, intense, dry, drained of true empathy.

"I told them to come. I told them to build the nest."

"What nest?"

"The nest on the chimney. When we die, the birds will take us to Jesus. I wanted us all to be with Jesus in heaven. Mr. Burkin told me, 'Only the infidels. Only your parents and Phillip go now. You stay behind. You are chosen.'" Adrienne tears up. "I wanted to go with Mommy and Daddy and Phillip to see Grandma and Grandpa Reynolds in heaven. Mr. Burkin said no. He said I had to stay and command the eagles. He said I had to wait to join Gramma and Grampa and Mommy and Daddy and Phillip in heaven. He said it wouldn't hurt."

Humming. Rocking. Tears streak the child's pale cheeks.

"So I did it. I said the words Mr. Burkin taught me. I made the birds come. I didn't want to do it, but Mr. Burkin said I had to. He said I'd die if I didn't say them, and I'd go to hell. He said I'd never see Mommy and Daddy and Phillip in heaven."

Adrienne smiles. A strange secret smile. "I told the birds where to find us. The birds took Mommy and Daddy and Phillip to heaven. I'll go to heaven soon. The eagles will take me. They will lift me up on eagles' wings."

Police Report, November 7, 2005: Autopsy on the bodies of Gina and Thomas Reynolds and their eight-year-old son, Phillip. The Reynolds family died of accidental carbon monoxide poisoning when an eagle's nest blocked their cabin's stone fireplace. The sole survivor, Adrienne Reynolds, age ten, has been incoherent since the event.

Circle Seven: the Violent

VIOLENCE AGAINST NEIGHBORS in the bloody River Phlegethon.

Violence against self in the Wood of Suicides.

Violence against God, Art and Nature on the burning sand.

Two stories, one of violence by a serial killer, one of violence directed against the self…

Going Through Hell

"If you're going through hell, keep on going."
– Winston Churchill

KERRY STRAIT STRUGGLED AGAINST THE HANDCUFFS that bound her to the concrete block wall. She knew she'd been half-propped, half-hanging here, a prisoner, since yesterday. Yesterday, the day before All Hallow's Eve, a night that, according to ancient custom, is a feast of the dead, a day when the dead can return to the land of the living to celebrate with their families.

Kerry wasn't dead yet. And she sure wasn't celebrating. Her wrists were numb and bleeding, her face bruised from the unsuccessful struggle with the assailant who had carried her to this hiding place. She was tired, dirty, petrified. She smelled of urine and perspiration. The basement itself reeked. Cold. Damp. A moldy odor. Small chirping, scuffling noises convinced her that rats or mice were her sole companions.

Kerry was freezing. She was clad only in a pink lacy size 38C Victoria's Secret bra and matching panties, the underwear she'd been sleeping in when she was kidnapped. She had been too tired after work to walk to the bathroom where her nightgown hung on a hook. She had removed her uniform and shoes, thrown them on the closet floor, and fallen into bed and deep slumber.

Just a few hours, she told herself at the time. *Then I'll get up, clean up, write.* Writing was what had gotten her into this predicament in the first place. Her own fault. Who did she think she was? Mary Shelley? The female version of Joseph Wambaugh? What made her think that her single

101

year on the force or being editor of her high school newspaper made a potential novelist of a ninety-five pound, size-four rookie policewoman? Visions of "Hill Street Blues" or "NYPD Blue" must have been dancing in her head.

All that was dancing in her head now were horrifying images of the Jack-O-Lantern killer's twelve previous victims, all killed precisely at midnight on Halloween over the past twelve years. It was Kerry's case. She'd been poring over the photos in the station house for months. Gory. Mesmerizing. Was she to be the unlucky 13th victim? Was Jose Ramirez the perp she'd been tracking for six months? *Stellar police work, Kerry*, she thought. *You'll surely get a Mayoral Citation for this crack bit of Sherlock Holmes sleuthing.*

It had all started when she'd answered an ad in "Writer's Review:" **"Writers wanted to develop seed ideas. Payment in advance for writer selected. "** A phone number followed. Foolishly, Kerry the Cop answered the ad. Then she committed an even bigger error. She revealed she was a woman writer who lived alone. She didn't mention her police background, but stressed her writing credentials—some would say exaggerated her writing credentials. A man who called himself "Jose" told her a tale so weird it had to be true.

"My mother used to be electrologist," he said on the phone in heavily accented Spanish-influenced English. "Do you know what thees is…thees electrologist word?"

Kerry thought she did. To be sure, she answered, "Why don't you tell me?"

"She remove unwanted body hair from customers. Many years she do thees in Mexico City. The customers, they tell her things. Some of the things…they very weird. Sexual. Kinky. You are not offended writing about thees?" asked Jose. "The writer we want will have to write about sexual stuff because these customers, they tell my mother many tales. Sometimes the tales, they very weird. Sometimes homosexual. You're not offended by gays? You don't mind writing about those who like to be dominated? Some of the stories she knows, they are about alien witchcraft rituals. My mother, she believe in this very much. Mama was taken up in a spacecraft once. Horrible alien witchcraft rituals…they were performed on her. She was just a young girl at the time."

"I am open-minded." What else did you say to someone telling you about alien abduction, his mother, electrolysis and sex in the same conversation? Kerry was spooked by Jose's weird frankness on the phone. But he offered her a lot of money. It checked out that he had been a surgeon in Mexico City. For an unsuccessful writer who could paper her bedroom with rejection notices, a solid offer to write anything for a substantial sum of cash was tempting.

Now that Kerry was Jose's prisoner, it was clear that Jose Ramirez had been into some nasty shit for years. From Kerry's study of the Jack-O-Lantern Killer as one of the investigating team, Kerry knew he carved women up with surgical precision. Jack the Ripper had nothing on Jack-O-Lantern. The only victim who had ever escaped, Jane Leslie, told police that her captor wore a mask and did not speak to her while she was imprisoned. He had enjoyed humiliating her and making her humiliate him. While raping her, over and over again, with a variety of objects, he chanted, "May I, Mommy? May I, Mommy?"

From Jane's account, Kerry knew it was her role in this charade to say, "Yes, you may, Jose." This would minimize the use of foreign objects. At least, according to Jane, it would be more likely that Jose would penetrate her primarily with his penis or a dildo, rather than some of the gruesome artifacts he employed on Jane before she escaped. Kerry had been slapped repeatedly until she could repeat the phrase without sobbing. Her police training helped. She found herself able to analyze her situation and do what Jose asked. Don't panic. Always try to survive, rape victims were told. Try to remember every detail of your attacker. Don't struggle if you're helpless. Don't beg for mercy. That's exactly what the rapist wants: control. Jose wanted her to beg for mercy. Kerry wouldn't beg. There was some connection, in Jose's warped mind, anyway, between the murders and alien witchcraft rituals. *Maybe raping me is one of those alien rituals?* Kerry thought through the haze of pain and hunger. Her sense of humor kicked in. *I'll bet Jose really is an illegal alien.*

Jose had continued, during that initial phone conversation. "My mother and I…we need to know, from a writer, whether these stories, whether they are short stories? A collection? Or maybe longer. Maybe a novel? Mama always want to write about what she say happened to her as young girl in Mexico. Aliens practice witchcraft on her, take her in their space machine? Can you advise us? If you can, and we like you, we hire you and sign a contract: six figures, plus a large advance. You will take my mother's life stories and write them? I was a doctor in Mexico City. I have money."

Why had this sounded plausible at the time? Actually, it had not. Aliens? Witchcraft? Kerry had checked, however, and a Dr. Jose Ramirez, a surgeon, *was* listed in Mexico City. (She wondered if that name was as common as Smith in the US?) Six figures was a lot of money to a Chicago cop. From there, she assumed that Dr. Ramirez really did have the money. She humored him, even though torn between laughing at his offer and crying that her writing career was reduced to this. But she couldn't afford to offend Jose, so she said, "Tell you what, Jose. I can't offer my professional judgment until I know what some of these stories are. Why don't you send me one or two of your mother's most interesting stories by E-mail? I'll get back to you." This seemed a good solution to the problem and, after all, what harm could looking at his mother's rough drafts do?

"We do not have a computer, Ms. Strait. My mother, she ees old-fashioned. You must geeve me your mailing address."

How dumb could one wanna-be writer be? *Pretty damn dumb*, she thought, struggling against her restraints for the thousandth time, mind reeling. *I should've gotten a post office box. Yeah. Right. I get soooo many offers from psychotic guys wanting my address to hire me to work on their writing*, she thought. *Happens all the time.*

Once he knew her home address, Jose came to her ground floor condo apartment in the dim hours of dawn. He picked the lock, entered, chloroformed her as she slept, carried her off to a roller skating rink. Physically removing the slight girl wasn't that difficult for a full-grown man. Imprisoned now, the far-away sound of skaters overhead and the merry music wafting downstairs made the entire experience even stranger. *This is surreal as hell*, she thought. How she wished she could take back the moment when she had actually given this pervert her real home address.

Whenever Jose came downstairs to check on her, the smell of hot buttered popcorn wafted down the stairs to the hungry prisoner. The smell made her empty stomach feel emptier still. The greasy buttery smell sickened her. She hadn't eaten or slept in over forty-eight hours. The old battered school-style black clock mounted high on the wall opposite Kerry told her it was 11:00 p.m. Halloween night. She felt as nauseous as if she'd actually eaten buckets of the greasy canola-oil coated popcorn she could smell. An inner voice warned: *Time is running out. You've got to make your move. You've got to get out of here. Now!*

But Jose wanted to talk. On his first visit to her dank dungeon, in broken English Jose had told her the sad story of his life. How he had once been a successful surgeon in Mexico City until a car accident took his right hand, leaving him with a gleaming metal prosthesis. He spoke of his move to Chicago, where he opened a skating rink because the Ramirez family had relatives here.

"I love to skate," Jose told Kerry. "A person can still skate with just one good hand. You no do surgery with a hook, but I skate good," said Jose.

Kerry nodded, not wanting to piss off the pervert. *Nothing worse than a pissed-off pervert*, she thought, inwardly amused by the alliteration.

Every Halloween for the past twelve years, Jose had carved a jack-o-lantern from a young female victim, claiming that alien witchcraft rituals required that it be done. Each U.S. victim had come to him from an ad placed in the writing magazine. There was really no other connection among the dead girls. He picked the smallest ones, who could be carried more easily. Coincidentally, they were all brunettes. Since some of the victims had been killed in Mexico City, before Jose moved north, that was logical. The police had not figured out the connection between the United States victims. A few dead Mexico City victims didn't merit their attention. *If I live, I can fill them in, Kerry thought. I'll get a gold star and a citation. Big whoop!* She spat coppery blood from her thirsty, aching mouth.

One year, when he was still in Mexico City, Jose had used only the victim's skull for his handiwork. He placed a flashlight inside Janice Ravera's hollowed-out skull, which made for a totally eerie police find. His first year in Chicago he carved a happy face in Judy Booth's abdomen, the grin oozing bloody gore downward towards her mons pubis. Another year, he cut a frown face in Brenda Womack's chest, removed her heart, and cut the rib-cage with the same surgical saw he had once used while performing open-heart surgeries in Mexico. Brenda provided a canvas for his creativity. This was when the police knew that their serial killer had some medical training. But the cops weren't looking for doctors hiding out in roller skating rinks.

After Jose lost his hand in Mexico City in the auto accident, his descent into madness and perversion, fueled by a fondness for sado-masochistic sex, accelerated. He liked whips. He liked chains. He liked whips *and* chains. He told one victim, "It is better to geeve than to receive," as he forced her to beat him with a studded whip until he bled. Pain was pleasure; pleasure, pain.

Jose had control issues and Mother issues. When he used his mother's electrolysis stories, he was fabricating, but Jose's relationship with his mother was definitely not normal. Jose was about as normal as the Night Stalker. Tales of alien witchcraft rituals dominated his earliest childhood memories, related to him by his deranged, drug-addled mother and internalized by the young boy from age five on.

Now it was Kerry receiving hourly beatings, imprisoned, pinioned on this hellish wall, a live butterfly squirming on a pin. She'd been chained in this dank basement for hours, listening to the deranged music from the roller skating rink above, fearing the return of the swarthy man who planned to kill her at midnight on Halloween, just as he had killed all the others. He'd leave her body in some remote location for the police to find. Kerry was the police officer working on the case; she knew all the gory details. Ironic.

Just out of reach on a nearby table Jose's surgical instruments waited. The instruments with which he had carved and cut and laid bare flesh and sinew, leaving human jack-o-lanterns in place of beautiful young girls. All the victims were petite brunettes, would-be writers who never lived to write another word. Kerry planned to live to write this story. *Great material for a horror novel here*, she thought. *Probably be rejected: too far-out.* She could imagine the rejection notice now: *"Do serial killer guys really spend this much time talking to their prisoners? I doubt it. Now, if you could work on something more believable. Perhaps a roller-skating clown trips, falls downstairs, and comes to Kerry's rescue?"* Kerry smiled to quell her fear.

With the beacon of survival and her urge for self-preservation spurring her on, Kerry wriggled her right hand until it cramped violently. Her right wrist was double-jointed, an old intramural basketball injury from high school. She could wriggle her right hand out of the restraints, but she knew she could not do so with her uninjured left hand. She worked against the pain until, crying aloud, her wrist slipped from the shackles. Wriggling it to restore the circulation, she realized that her left wrist remained imprisoned, firmly pinioned against the cold, pebbly concrete, the metal handcuffs and circular chains attached and embedded in the concrete block wall.

Kerry saw the gleaming instruments on the table. Arranged, waiting for midnight when the roller skating rink would close. Jose would descend, mumble words of ancient alien witchcraft rituals. Then he would slice her to shreds. She remembered the way the light glinted crazily off the hook where Jose's right hand had been as he violated her, again and again, with every imaginable implement, not just his own sometimes-inadequate penis. Every hour of her imprisonment was a living hell. The clock's hands ticked towards 11:15 p.m.

The horror of Jose's metal hook gave Kerry an idea, an idea just crazy enough to save her life, if she had the resolve, the constitution to follow through with it. Kerry remembered the young mountain climber who had amputated his own arm, tied a tourniquet around the stump, and climbed down a mountainside to safety. If she could reach the table on wheels that held Jose's hellish surgical instruments, she, too, could cut off her own left hand, tie a tourniquet, and escape out the basement window to safety. All that was required was the desire to live and the resolve not to pass out from pain. She was sure she could reach the wheeled instrument table with her left foot. Her right hand was now free. Her bra could serve as a tourniquet.

Now is not the time for modesty, Kerry reasoned. *What other choices do I have? I'm running out of time.*

She strained, gritting her teeth. The table on wheels moved. Imperceptible, at first, it inched its way towards her. It almost toppled. Kerry held her breath. Sweat trickled down her brow, obscuring her vision. She gasped. A pent-up breath. She stretched toward the table. It seemed impossibly far away. Then the surgical steel knife was in her grasp, its metal cold in her sweaty fingers. Kerry took a deep breath and cut shallowly into her left wrist.

The pain was excruciating. She thought she would faint. Involuntarily, she screamed in agony. It was dangerous to make any excessive noise, but the loud music blaring in the roller rink above drowned out her anguished cry.

Must be careful. Must not bleed to death. Should have tied bra around upper forearm before I cut. Shit! Why didn't I think of the tourniquet earlier? Because I was in shock, naked, shivering from the cold, dehydration and fear? Forced to listen to some weirdo spout tales about aliens in his backyard performing witchcraft on his mother. You think that could explain it?

Kerry wriggled her right arm out of the bra strap. Using the sharp surgical steel knife, she sliced the bra strap on her left shoulder. With her right hand and her teeth, she tied the tattered pink elastic bra as tightly as she could around her upper forearm, to guard against fatal hemorrhaging.

The first cut is not the deepest, she thought. Grim humor. *A good thing, since I was so stupid to cut before tying the tourniquet.* When you're going through hell, keep on going. That was Kerry Strait's goal: to keep on going.

Kerry made a second, less tentative cut where she had only nicked the skin before. She would need to break the hand at the wrist and saw through the cartilage. She tried with all her strength and determination, the smell of her own blood making her nauseous. *By God I'm not going to be anyone's Halloween jack-o-lantern.*

The sound! The sound of metal on bone, of knife on gristle.

She had once asked her good friend Bettie, a surgical nurse, "What was the worst surgery at which you ever assisted?" The response had surprised Kerry.

"A knee operation," Bettie had answered.

"Why a knee operation? Why not open heart surgery. Something like that?"

"The sound. The sound was godawful!"

And now that same godawful cutting, ripping, cartilage-destroying sound filled Kerry's ears. The difference between Bettie's casual observation to her years earlier and now: this was personal. *I'm attached to this wrist…in more ways than one.* When she thought about what she was doing, she almost fainted. She tried to pretend she was watching this being done to someone else. *Stand outside your body. Pretend it's someone else.*

But, now, finally, she was done. She was free. She tottered away from the wall, towards the half window high on the basement wall. Outside, a dark alley.

Climb to that window. Use the stool. Wriggle to freedom. Can I do it? Do I have enough left? Hell, yes!

Blood was trickling from the bloody stump, coating her stomach, her thighs. Her body was covered in her own blood, her empty stomach queasy. Kerry Strait was determined to survive.

I'm not dying because of some psychotic weirdo. I am not. I will not. Hell, no!

Carrie balanced her spiraling thoughts like a juggler using bruised peaches. Drop one; ruin it. Already hurting Big Time, as she teetered on the stool to reach the window, she looked back at the shackle that still held her severed left hand. *Can I take my hand with me? Should I climb back down and get it?* She heard a little old lady's voice in her head, saying, *"Why, certainly, dear. And, while you're at it, run upstairs and get some popcorn to eat with your remaining right hand."* She shook her head to regain rational thought. *Do you really think that gory lump you're looking at can be re-attached? Get real! You'll climb down there; he'll come back; it'll be curtains. Suck it up! You did an amazingly bad job removing that hand, by the way. It's toast. Get over it already. And get the hell out of here!*

It was 11:45 p.m on Halloween night. At midnight her life would end. *This is it. Now or never. This is my only chance. I'm not going to become anybody's jack-o-lantern. I'm going through hell, but I'm going to keep right on going.*

Oozing blood, she continued her climb out the half-window high up on the wall of the basement. A collection of full garbage bags in the alley below cushioned her clumsy fall to the pavement. Adrenaline pumping, Kerry struggled up from the blood-slick vinyl bags, regained her feet and ran as though the devil himself were after her.

When Kerry made book-signing tours across the country to publicize her best-selling novel, *Jailing Jack,* she'd describe her escape and rescue. Then she'd quote Winston Churchill one more time, "If you're going through hell, keep on going!"

Living in Hell

IT WAS TAD'S EIGHTH BIRTHDAY PARTY, and his parents had spared no expense.

"We've got Pogo the Clown coming," Mrs. McGreevy told her friend Sally. "He's the best clown in Waterloo, Iowa. Everybody says he makes really good balloon animals. Pogo did the Chandlers' party at their house, but this party is going to make the Chandlers' party look like the Screw-Up at the OK Corral."

Jeannie McGreevy hated Cassie Chandler. She had hated Cassie ever since she realized that Cassie was just leeching off her, using her to obtain summer jobs for her daughter, Belinda.

Sally took another sip of her frozen Margarita at Applebee's.

"That sounds really nice, Jeannie. Is Tad excited about the party? I mean…does he want to have a clown and fifty guests?"

Tad McGreevy's frail health and generally weird demeanor were well known amongst the McGreevy's neighbors and friends. Tad was always just a little bit…. different. It wasn't just his androgynous appearance, although he did look "too pretty to be a boy," as many admirers had said of Jeannie McGreevy's son when they saw him in his stroller on the street as an infant.

Since those halcyon stroller days, Tad had grown into a third-grader with a "sensitive" stomach, who sometimes cried for no apparent reason. This made him the butt of other kids' mean-spirited jokes, and many times he had come home from school with a bloody nose, courtesy of some Waterloo redneck. His mother was always telling him not to be so sensitive, but Tad was Tad.

111

While Sally's husband, Earl Scranton, worked at Rath Packing Plant, slaughtering hogs and cattle with a stun gun on long 12-hour shifts, Jim McGreevy was a lawyer who charged $300 an hour. It was easy to envy the McGreevys. They seemed to have it all: the big house, the cute well-behaved children (Tad and his older sister, twelve-year-old Sharon.)

Jeannie McGreevy was also a size zero. That, alone, made other women hate her. Sally, herself, was just being a friend of Jeannie's so that Shannon Scranton could benefit. Sharon's old school uniforms fit Sally's daughter, Shannon, perfectly, and Jeannie McGreevy always gifted her good friend Sally Scranton with them, free and gratis, for the Catholic school that both girls attended, where Shannon was one year behind Sharon. Shannon and Sharon were on the same volleyball team. The Scrantons didn't have a lot of extra cash; every little bit helped.

Sally commented to her husband, Earl, who was splattered with pigs' blood from working the late shift at Rath, "I wonder if Tad McGreevy might be autistic. He doesn't say much and he seems so weird. He's got no social skills. Maybe he has that deal where the kid is really smart, but really strange…that Ashburger's Syndrome. Something like what Dustin Hoffman had in that movie."

Earl Scranton was no genius, but he corrected Sally, who was still slurring her words after having drunk ten margaritas at Applebee's on Jeannie McGreevy's dime, saying, "It's Asperger's Syndrome, and Tad McGreevy is just a weird dork." Earl toweled off with the kitchen dishtowel (always a sticking point with Sally) and headed towards the bedroom to change his clothes, thinking to himself that his wife, Sally, was a moron. Marrying her because she had been pregnant with little Steven had not been one of his smarter moves.

The Saturday of Tad's party dawned cool and drizzly. It was late April. April in Iowa can be unpredictable.

Pogo the Clown had a day job. Pogo, also known as Michael Clay, ran his father-in-law's chicken restaurant, Mike's Chicken Shack, by night, and took paying clown gigs by day, on weekends. Pogo's costume was classic clown: big shoes, red hair, striped baggy pants, white pancake make-up, and a large red smile reaching towards his ears. Pogo would be a hit; Jeannie just knew it. She smiled to herself, thinking how much better *her* party would be than the one that Sally Chandler had thrown for little Susie Chandler last fall. Of course, the Chandlers had even more money than the McGreevys and Sally had rented Black's Tea Room for her daughter's party, but Jeannie McGreevy figured, "It's April and kids want to be outside, running around. Our back yard will do just fine."

Pogo arrived at the McGreevy residence in Cedar Falls, Iowa, at ten o'clock in the morning on April 24th. Cedar Falls was where all the upwardly mobile people in town lived. Waterloo was strictly blue-collar and largely black. The unincorporated township of Deer Run, Iowa, just across the street from the Rath Packing Plant, was even lower on the totem pole than Waterloo.

Sally Sloan lived in Waterloo—not quite as bad as Deer Run—but she'd met Jeannie McGreevy at the school their sons both attended, Rossdale Elementary. Iowa is a school choice state. The Scrantons had selected Rossdale in order to get the best possible public school education for young Steven, who was bussed twenty miles to and from school every morning and afternoon. They were paying for Stevie's older sister, Shannon, to go to a private Catholic school, because Shannon was smart.

Rossdale was a good public school, good enough for Stevie. Probably better than Stevie deserved, since he wasn't much of a scholar, but getting him to and from Rossdale Elementary really screwed up the family's schedule.

When Tad first saw Pogo, standing there on his front stoop in full clown make-up, Tad turned a strange pale chalky color that rivaled the whiteness of Pogo's pancake make-up. Although Tad always looked pallid, his red curly hair became damp and curled wetly against his pale freckled cheeks, dripping with sudden sweat. Tad began to breathe heavily as he backed away from the approaching clown, retreating to the safety and security of the house, sinking down next to the large aquarium that the family kept in the middle of the family room.

"What's the matter, honey? You look like you're gonna' be sick," Jeannie said. No sooner had the words left her mouth then the Fritos Tad had consumed before the party left his stomach, splattering the back of Jeannie McGreevy's pale white couch. Mrs. McGreevy ushered Tad into the bathroom to clean him up. When he emerged from the family's bathroom, Tad was carrying his asthma inhaler and puffing on it like it was a cigarette and he was experiencing nicotine withdrawal. Jeannie McGreevy, in a peeved voice, was saying to Tad, as she ushered him back into the family room, "Why couldn't you have thrown up in the fish tank, instead of on my new couch?" Pogo was gone. He was outside, socializing with the guests and entertaining the children. He seemed especially fond of the little boys at the party.

"Tad, you look like you've seen a ghost!" said his classmate, Stevie Scranton, mouth agape, when Tad finally emerged from the house, slowly and hesitantly, to join his own party, in progress.

In fact, Tad *had* seen a ghost, of sorts. He had seen an aura surrounding Michael Clay, a pale color, like gray-green decomposing dead flesh, that overshadowed Pogo's white clown. Tad saw "auras," that is colors, around all people. Yellow meant the person was good. Red meant they were prone to be violent. Black meant that they were ill and would die soon or die young. Vivid emerald green was one of the best, health-wise, but Tad preferred the yellows, who were always kind, compassionate, giving souls. Tad's mom was a pink: verging on red, but too timid to be dangerously violent His dad, Jim, was a blue, remote and indifferent to the plight of others. Pretty much a self-contained entity with little time for emotional output towards others.

But gray-green was the worst. The absolute worst. Tad had only ever seen one person with that dangerous khaki color before, and that was on television. His aura was so strong that the "X" on Charles Manson's forehead barely made an impression on the sensitive young boy watching a documentary on late-night television about the long-ago killings of a movie star and her friends. At the time, the baby-sitter was making out with her boyfriend in the next room.

Tad never told anyone about the colors he saw; people already thought he was weird, and his parents would never believe him, anyway. It was just something he knew about people: whether they were "bad" or "good." The auras told him. The colors told him.

"D—d—don't make me go near him," Tad gasped to Stevie. "Tell my mom I'm gonna' urp again." Stevie knew Tad meant the clown, without asking.

Hearing that Tad might spew again, Stevie Scranton backed up ten paces, but, unlike Tad, later on, outside, playing in the yard, he was happy to receive a balloon animal shaped like an elephant from Pogo. Stevie sat on Pogo's lap while Pogo made the brightly colored balloon animal for him, the air filled with squeaking sounds as Pogo twisted and tied the plastic pachyderm into shape(s). The other kids were rioting merrily in the cool spring air. Tad sat apart, looking miserable, seated on the back yard swing set. Tad refused to go anywhere near Pogo the Clown. Jeannie McGreevy was heard muttering to Sally, "Well, there's one hundred bucks down the drain!"

The bad dreams began two days later.

Tad woke in the night screaming. "The fish! The fish! There's a skull in the aquarium!"

Jim and Jeannie McGreevy ran to Tad's room, comforted him, asked him what he was talking about. Tad was incoherent. His tale of skulls and fish and an aquarium made no sense to them. Even taking Tad downstairs and showing him the aquarium in the family room, resting on the couch table behind Jeannie's now-stained white couch did not comfort Tad. His eyes looked wide and frightened.

The second dream occurred the next night. Tad screamed so loudly that it actually woke the neighbors. He described having a crucifix stuffed down his throat. "I don't know why I had to swallow the crucifix," he said. "It hurt. It hurt a lot." To further intensify the impact of this story, Tad had bitten through his lip. Flecks of blood flew from his mouth as he spoke.

The third night, Tad cried out at three in the morning.

"What is it this time?" said Jeannie McGreevy to her son, wearily.

"It was a man, Mom. A black man. His body was all cut up, all carved up. He was half-in and half-out of a bathtub. His heart was gone. I think he ate it."

"Who ate it?" Jeannie McGreevy was exhausted after three days with little sleep, and Tad's tales were becoming gorier and making even less sense.

"The clown. The clown ate it."

"What clown? You mean Pogo?"

"Yes. He ate it. He cut the boy's chest open and took the heart out and ate it. It was still beating when he ate it." Tad choked back vomit. His shivering was pitiful, but the McGreevy's were fast losing patience.

"Todd! You've got to get a grip! There's no clown. There's no killer. You're just having a bad dream. You've got to quit waking all of us up in the middle of the night like this!" That was Jim McGreevy, sounding angry. The family returned to their beds, weary from another night of Tad's imaginative nightmares. Their patience was wearing thin. Tad's sister, Sharon, had just put a pillow over her head and stayed locked in her room.

Tad looked peaked, too. Every single day, he looked as though he had been up all night. Some nights, that was true. After his parents and sister returned to their beds and to slumber, Tad was afraid to sleep, afraid of what dreams might bring.

After seven nights of terrifying visions, most of them making little or no sense when the frightened boy related them to his concerned parents, Jeannie and James McGreevy made an appointment for Tad with the best children's psychiatrist in Cedar Falls, Iowa. Dr. Eisenstadt was expensive, but he would be worth it. It had been ten days since Tad's birthday party, and Tad had had ten nightmares in a row, each one more horrifying than the last. Nobody was sleeping much at the McGreevy household, and everyone was on edge.

Dr. Eisenstadt tried to take Tad's arm in a friendly fashion and guide him from the waiting room into his inner office, but Tad pulled away from the white-haired man with the black aura in alarm. Jeannie McGreevy rose to accompany Tad into the doctor's office.

Dr. Eisenstadt said, "Please...no...it is best if Tad and I begin the process alone."

For the next hour, Tad poured out gory tale after gory tale. Body parts in vats of acid. Heads in the refrigerator. Skulls boiled and then painted. Beating hearts taken from victims and eaten cannibalistically by a crazed killer.

"Who is killing all these people, Tad?" asked Dr. Eisenstadt. "Do you know this man?"

"Yes, Dr. Eisenstadt," the young boy said, somberly. "It's the clown. He's a killer. He even said, 'If you're a clown, you can get away with murder.'"

Dr. Eisenstadt conferred with Mr. and Mrs. McGreevy after Tad's second week in treatment. It had been twenty-five days (and nights) since Tad's party and there had been twenty-five nightmares.

No one in the McGreevy house was getting any sleep, but giving Tad sleeping pills just seemed to make matters worse. Not only did Tad still wake up screaming, but, the next day, he was zombie-like in school. One teacher even saw him stagger and sway in the hallway and had to quickly run to catch him before he fell. It was obvious that the various drug therapies that were being tried on the young boy were a case of the cure being as bad or worse than the disease.

"I have one more suggestion," said Dr. Eisenstadt, after thirty days of treatment.

"What, Doctor? We'll do anything, pay anything. We are all suffering." Jim McGreevy summed up the family's ordeal, night after night. Jim wanted to say, "Enough already! I need to get some sleep!" All of the McGreevys, to use an old clichéd expression, looked as though they had been "rode hard and put away wet."

"Obviously, young Tad is suffering from some form of delusion that centers on the clown, Pogo, who performed at his eighth birthday party. Now, we all know that Tad is imagining these horrible murders and all the other unspeakable things he describes. But drug therapy isn't working, and Tad keeps maintaining that *we* are the deluded ones and *he* is the only sane one. He told me, at our last session, 'I see his aura. It's gray-green, Dr.

Eisenstadt. Only the worst of the worst are gray-green.' Tad claims that people have 'auras' and he can see these colors around his classmates and teachers and family and friends. In essence, he is saying that he is able to see into the souls of all those around him. Now, I know this is silly, but Tad really believes it." Dr. Eisenstadt released a pent-up sigh. "I think I've done about as much for him as I can."

"Is Tad crazy?" asked Jeannie McGreevy, tears welling up in her eyes.

"We don't like to use the term 'crazy.' Tad has some mental issues. I am unable to determine, here, whether he is obsessive-compulsive, paranoid-schizophrenic, or any of a variety or combination of other more complicated mental conditions. You really should check him into Shady Oaks for evaluation. They can do a more complete diagnosis, a more complete medical work-up. Maybe there is an abnormality of the brain? A tumor, perhaps? An MRI could determine this, but I don't have the necessary equipment here in the office to diagnose Tad's problem. I suggest a one-week stay in Shady Oaks."

Tad entered Shady Oaks the next day. It had been thirty days since his birthday party. Thirty days of screaming, night terrors and wild tales of cannibalism, murder, skulls, aquariums and violence. In one dream, from which Tad woke shaking uncontrollably, he described the killer trepanning his victim, attempting to keep a nineteen-year-old victim alive for days, making holes in the young man's head and repeatedly raping the young male subject as the hapless victim lay in a near-coma in Pogo's bathroom bathtub.

It was this last story that made Jeannie McGreevy physically gag and run to the bathroom. After that, Jeannie dropped her objections to committing Tad to the clinic on a trial basis for a week. Originally, she had said, "What will the neighbors say?"

Her husband replied, "They'll probably say: good. Now we can get through one entire night without screaming coming from the McGreevys' house." Personally, James McGreevy was looking forward to getting a good night's sleep, his first in over a month.

Jeannie muttered, to her husband, "Another three thousand dollars down the drain," as they walked out of Dr. Eisenstadt's office.

Tad entered the clinic on a Saturday, thirty days after his birthday party.

He quit speaking. He quit eating. He stared blankly into space and would not answer any questions. He seemed to have had a total break with reality. He was delusional, locked within his own private world now.

The McGreevys had to take turns spoon-feeding him a soft diet, since Tad wouldn't feed himself and barely chewed his food. He resembled a 90-year-old more than a nearly-9-year-old.

On the 33rd day after his eighth birthday party, the local papers in Waterloo, Iowa carried the front-page story of the arrest of Michael Clay, a local businessman who ran Mike's Chicken Shack for his father-in-law and moonlighted, on weekends, as Pogo the Clown. The papers reported that thirty-three bodies had been found buried beneath Pogo's house and others had been found in various stages of decomposition in a basement bathroom. The descriptions of what the victims had endured before death were very disturbing.

Early accounts confirmed nearly all the details that young Tad had poured out during his night terrors. Skulls had been boiled, penises cut off and kept in jars of formaldehyde. Two policemen threw up when they opened a refrigerator and found two severed heads inside. The picture of the nude man, bound to what looked like a dentist's chair and headless, was widely distributed on the Internet. The body in the bathtub was just as Tad had described it to his disbelieving family.

The McGreevys conferred with Dr. Eisenstadt, who agreed that young Tad should leave Shady Oaks and return home. Tad had been right about Pogo. This provided little real consolation to the family or to the boy. There was guilt, of course, that none of them had listened more closely or believed Tad's stories, but who could have known? Who would believe an eight-year-old who said he saw into peoples' souls? The hope now was that returning Tad to the bosom of his family, would help return him to some semblance of normalcy, since his time in Shady Oaks seemed to have made him worse.

Returned to familiar surroundings, Tad seldom spoke. He didn't answer when spoken to. He rarely smiled or showed any sign of even knowing that others were present in the room. When in his bedroom, he rocked back and forth, holding himself, knees to chest, moaning softly and that was the most emotion Tad displayed. He slept only fitfully, if at all. The dreams stopped, though. Although Tad mostly lay in bed staring at the ceiling, the screaming and night terrors seem to have stopped with the last of the murders.

Sometimes, Tad would be brought downstairs to the family room, in the futile hope that he would, once again, communicate with his family. He spent hours staring at the Puffer Fish in the aquarium. When Tad looked into the eerily human eyes of the Puffer Fish, Tad's own eyes held a look of indescribable terror. Thirty-three days. Thirty-three nights. Thirty-three victims. The Puffer fish stared back at the mute boy with its large, expressionless vacant eyes, silent, disconnected, aimlessly wandering in an aquarium limbo.

Circle Eight: the Fraudulent

CIRCLE NUMBER EIGHT HOLDS panderers, seducers, grafters, hypocrites, sowers of discord, fortunetellers, flatterers, falsifiers. In other words, it holds your neighbor and mine....

Listen to my tale of a doctor who is not what he represents to the world. And what if you, Gentle Reader, sought out this doctor for help?

Confessions of an Apotemnophile

APOTEMNOPHILIA. WHAT-THE-HELL IS *THAT?* *Sounds like a breed of hippopotamus.* The word slid deliciously off my tongue as I sat in the waiting room, thumbing through the reference work the psychiatrist had given me.

Body integrity identity disorder. *What's that got to do with me? There's nothing wrong with me. Nothing that a little amputation won't fix, that is. I've wanted to be rid of my left leg, now, since I met my first amputee at the hospital with my mother when I was six years old.*

"What happened to your leg, Mister?" I asked. Mom was around the corner in the hospital, visiting Grandpa, who was in an oxygen tent. She had parked me on a bench near the elevator. She told me not to move a muscle before she entered the room where my grandfather lay dying. I think she was afraid that I would be too upset seeing my grandfather, since the end was near.

The stranger smiled. "It's a long story, little boy."

"That's okay. I'm waiting for my mom, anyway."

"I think your mother should be here if I'm going to tell you how I lost my leg. She might not approve of my story." He held his hands outstretched, in the universal gesture that means, "I'm sorry, but there's nothing I can do." Sort of a half-shrug, palms upward.

And so Mr. Burden, sitting in his wheelchair waiting for the elevator, did not tell me until much later how he had gone to the park that warm September day in Florida, sat cross-legged on the lawn, rested the shotgun on his right thigh, cocked the trigger and intentionally blown off his left leg. The shot caused little pain. He made sure of that by aiming the barrel at a pre-selected point on his knee. Blood and muscle were exposed everywhere. The lower leg was hanging only by a grisly thread of bone and tissue. He tied the tourniquet tightly enough around his upper thigh to keep from bleeding to death.

Mr. Burden, a retired architect, then reached for the cell phone, which he'd placed next to him before the blast, dialed 911, and summoned help. Today, as he sat in the wheelchair in this hospital, five feet from the bench where I waited for my mother, he was not about to tell me his story. I would only learn it later, in adulthood.

But *his* story became *my* story.

I couldn't stop thinking about the mysterious man and his missing leg. I kept looking at *my* left leg. When I returned home, I started tucking my left pant leg up under me, pretending that my left leg was gone.

"Gregory White! What are you doing?" Mom sounded mad.

"Just playing."

"Playing what?"

"Just playing around."

"Go outside and *really* play. Run around with the other boys. Quit that!" My mother walked back into the kitchen from my room. She seemed upset.

Let's face it: I was a strange kid. From the time I was six, I often thought of Mr. Burden and his missing limb, and I wished with all my heart that my own left leg were missing above the knee. I felt deep guilt at hating my left leg, but I couldn't rid myself of my loathing for it. I wanted it gone. Permanently. It was *my* burden.

For a long time, I thought I was the only one in the world with this bizarre desire. I felt deep guilt. I wanted this aberrant wish of mine to disappear. I wanted to be "normal." If Mr. Burden had told me what had happened to his leg, that day in the hospital, would it have made me feel more "normal," knowing that there were more of me? I don't know. Finally, I acted on my secret suppressed dream and contacted a physician. I was thirty years old.

"Doc, I want you to remove my left leg below the knee."

The physician looked startled. He glanced away from me.

"Is there something wrong with your leg?"

"Not that I know of."

The orthopedic surgeon took out a pad and scribbled the name Dr. Hans Frank, 210 West 42nd Street, Suite 703. Before he handed it to me, he said, "My agreeing to amputate a healthy limb would be crazy. It would be a violation of the Hippocratic oath. It would be tantamount to a paranoid-schizophrenic coming in here and telling me to 'talk to the other voices' in treating him. We all live by the credo, 'First do no harm.' You don't need a surgeon. You need a good psychiatrist."

Dr. Frank, in turn, recommended the article I was now reading in his waiting room, *Apotemnophilia,* sub-titled *"Two Cases of Self-demand Amputation As a Paraphilia."* The only promising thing about the article was that it was in *The Journal of Sex Research.* I'm sure Dr. Frank was a very good psychiatrist, but I didn't think I'd be a very good patient. I tossed the article in the glossy magazine towards the stack of reading material on the waiting room table. It hit the top of the untidy stack, and a small landslide of stacked-up magazines and papers slid noisily to the floor, causing the other patients in the waiting room to stare.

Embarrassed, I rose to leave, before I had even been seen.

I knew I was absolutely fine. I also thought that finding some other people like me would be helpful. That's how I met up with Paul Campagna on the Internet.

"The apotemnophilia group is divided into pretenders, devotees and wannabees, " Paul told me during our first phone conversation. Paul would stop to cough a deep smoker's cough every few minutes.

"What's the difference?

"A pretender just wants to make a person think he's disabled. He uses a wheelchair or crutches. Stuff like that."

"OK. What's a devotee do?"

"A devotee is sexually attracted to people who have had amputations."

"Really?"

"Really," said Paul.

"And wannabees?"

"Wannabees get the most attention. They really and truly live for the removal of the healthy limb. You and I are wannabees. Do you want to do something about it?"

Paul suggested meeting at a small run-down bar, Sammy's Place, halfway between his home and mine. We met there, Sinatra bleating "My Way" in the background, drowning out the few bar patrons present, who were immersed in a blue smoky haze. When Paul asked me if I wanted to do something about our mutual affliction, he leaned forward, cigarette in hand, the ash on the end of his cigarette hovering perilously above my martini. There was a dangerous mesmerizing glint in his eye. I squirmed a bit on the red naugahyde bar stool, my butt making an embarrassing squeaking noise every time I repositioned myself.

Paul explained, "For me, sexuality is being comfortable with my body. In my mind, I feel like my legs don't belong to me. They shouldn't *be* there. My legs cause me to feel an overwhelming sense of despair." A heavy sigh followed that statement. The smoke from his cigarette spiraled towards the low ceiling of Sammy's place, as once again I carefully redistributed my weight on the bar stool.

I nodded my head in agreement with Paul's words about being comfortable in your own body and cracked a joke, "I'm just trying to get a leg up on this thing." Puns were my weakness. If Paul had no sense of humor, we were done.

But Paul smiled appreciatively and raised his martini glass to clink against mine, saying, "Touche!" We drank in silence for a moment, considering our mutual plight, me trying hard not to make that obnoxious squeaking noise again.

Paul was not as new to this disorder as I was. He'd been trying to convince a reputable doctor in his home state of Connecticut to amputate both of his legs for the past fifteen years. Paul had logged more shrink time on the couch than Woody Allen. Now he was sixty years old and he was just....ready.

"What can we do...if we're wannabees?" I asked Paul.

"I've been doing some research," Paul said. "There's supposed to be a doctor in Matamoras, just across the border from Brownsville, Texas, a Dr. Miguel Ortega. He'll perform the surgery, ...for a price."

"How much does he want?" I asked.

"Twenty thousand dollars per leg. It's ten thousand per leg."

I emitted a low whistle. Twenty thousand dollars was a fair chunk of change, but Paul was a wealthy attorney, and the insurance game had been good to me.

When we arrived in Matamoras, we searched for the doctor's office in the winding streets of the old city, near the Cathedral. The trees in the park across the street were festooned with winding, upward-spiraling strings of white lights, giving the town square a surreal Disneyland look. It was near Thanksgiving. When we couldn't find the doctor's office, I called his cell phone.

"I don't do the surgery in the office. I've recently moved," he told me on the phone. "Check into a suite at the brand new Holiday Inn on the edge of town

"But...you won't do the surgery there, will you?" I asked.

"Oh, yes. It's quite safe," he said. "Do you have the money?"

I quickly reassured Dr. Ortega that Paul had twenty thousand dollars for the removal of both of his legs, and I had ten thousand dollars for the removal of just my left leg. We proceeded to the Holiday Inn, as directed, and checked in. I used a fake name and paid cash.

The motel already had Christmas trees set up in the lobby, decorated with gold bows, even though it was only Thanksgiving. *Nothing like rushing the season*, I thought. And then I realized, *Christmas this year I won't have to live with my left leg.* I smiled for the first time since I had left home in New York, thinking what a nice early-season present that would be.

At the desk, we asked the clerk if she knew Dr. Ortega.

She looked away and then said, "Yes." Nothing more. She scurried from the desk and into the back room. Paul and I exchanged wary glances. Ominous.

After we had checked into our suites we met in the bar for a drink. Paul began chain-smoking immediately, as a plastic palm tree in the corner alternately lit up blue and then green, advertising an unfamiliar brand of Mexican tequila.

"I don't know, Paul. I'm not so sure about this," I said.

Paul sensed my uneasiness, but, by this point, he had adopted a certain fatalistic attitude. "Nothing ventured; nothing gained," he responded, stubbing out his omnipresent cigarette, shrugging and coughing as he did.

"What do we really know about this doctor? Is he any good? He's so secretive."

"Well, you understand why that is, don't you? He'd be arrested. No doctor in the United States will knowingly amputate a healthy limb. This doctor is from Brownsville, but he crosses the border to do the surgeries here, for fear he'll lose his license to practice medicine in the U.S."

"I understand that," I said, "but it's hardly confidence-inspiring."

"Look at it this way, Gregg. You don't have to go through with it, but it's now or never, for me. I've been this way for over twenty-five years. I just don't want to go on living this way any longer. Dr. Ortega has done many sexual reassignment surgeries. Compared to cutting off some guy's schlong, removing my sixty-year-old legs shouldn't be a big deal." Paul threw back another vodka martini and lit another cigarette.

Schlong. I smiled at the term.

And so it was that Paul's legs were surgically removed at the Holiday Inn in Matamoras, Mexico, at daybreak. During the night, I had a moment when I realized I just could not go through with my surgery. I had a nightmarish vision of bodiless legs marching towards the open fiery door of a crematorium. A smell of burning flesh from the dream limbs, as the disembodied appendages marched into oblivion, made me nauseous. I awakened in the dark…cold, clammy, and shivering like a Mexican hairless. I just was not as brave as Paul. Or maybe I was just not as desperate.

When I left, Paul was doped up on painkillers, groggily recuperating in his suite, two Mexican nurse's aides by his side. I squeezed his hand, wished him well, and left for the airport. I pocketed an OxyContin pill or two from the tray near his bed before I left.

One week later I read about the arrest of a Dr. Miguel Ortega in Brownsville. He was charged with murder after the body of a sixty-year-old man, Paul Campagna, was found in a suite at the Holiday Inn in Matamoras, Mexico. The victim had been dead for three days. Gangrene.

I put down the *USA Today*, stunned. *Paul! It's Paul! I can't even honor his memory by attending his funeral.* If anyone were to find out that I had been Paul's companion in Mexico, who knew what might happen? I could lose my job. Insurance agencies frown on their top agents running off to Mexico to have their healthy legs amputated. I could hear the water cooler talk now. *Thank God I paid cash and used an alias when I checked into that Holiday Inn.*

A few months passed, and my longing to become limbless grew more and more intense, like a festering sore. First, I contemplated killing my lower left leg by submerging it in a vat of dry ice. I'd read about a woman in Wales who had succeeded in doing that. After that, the doctors *had* to help her. Then it came to me.

I would follow the lead of the very first amputee I'd ever encountered: Mr. Burden. Only I wouldn't use a shotgun because, quite frankly, I feared I would lack the necessary courage to pull the trigger at the moment of truth. I had failed to pull the trigger in Matamoras, figuratively speaking.

I charged up my cell phone. I began drinking vodka martinis in the afternoon, in honor of Paul, and I popped a couple of Paul's purloined pills, smiling at the alliteration. I drove to a deserted area where the Amtrak schedule said a midnight train would come barreling through.

In anxious anticipation of the train, I tied a tourniquet above my left knee.

I'm finally ready to pull the trigger like Mr. Burden in the park. I'm so smashed I'm humming "Midnight Train to Georgia." Woozy. Wet grass beside the tracks stains my shirt. Cold steel beneath my leg, cooler now in the dead of night, comforts me. Home. Reminds me of home. Legs up on the metal handlebars of my bicycle. Rolling full-speed down Twelfth Street. Finally ready to roll. Full speed ahead. No more procrastinating. Time to pull the trigger. Time to board the train.

The train. The train. "Gonna' board the midnight train." I hate my leg. I hate my leg.

I'm an insect to the thundering metal beast. Excruciating pain. I bite through my lip to muffle my screams. Blood, wet grass soak me. Warm dew?

I reach down to embrace my bloody stump. Bought a one-way ticket...to insufferable pain...to agony...to joy. Cold, clammy skin. Sweaty hands. Anxiety. Confusion. Salty swallow floods my sinuses. Is it over? I'll be with him. I'd rather live in his world than live with legs in mine.

Death grip on phone. *Push the buttons.*

Far away, I hear a tinny, robotic, chilly repetitive monotone. *Please hang up and try your call again.*

Warm salty blood trickling down the back of my throat. Is this a simpler place and time, like in the song? Oh, yes it is. Oh, yes it is. Am I even here?

He said he'd be leavin'.

Gotta go. Gonna' board.

Circle Nine: Cocytus

THIS IS THE COLDEST PLACE IN HELL… the farthest away from human emotion and the deepest pit of suffering.

All is ice. Satan himself is trapped in ice. Rivers, trees, all is a frozen wasteland.

Cold as hell, cold as sin: Cocytus, the ninth circle of hell.

An American Girl*

1/21/2005, MILLERSBURG, ILLINOIS FIELD

Cody always looked to Rebecca for guidance. He looked to her now, standing there in the frigid winter dusk in a Millersburg, Illinois, field. It was January 21, 2005. Cody was holding a rusty gas can in his large calloused hands. He wore green cotton work gloves, but his fingers were as cold as ice, as cold as his heart.

Becky knew she had to remain strong. Cody was weak under pressure. She thrust her hands deep into the pockets of her blue parka. Her studded dog collar bracelet caught on the pocket as she inserted her right hand. She adopted her toughest badass sneer and tried to look impassive. The cold was intense. It felt as though all her metal piercings…ears, tongue, nipples, eyebrows…. were permanently freezing into every body orifice. The deeper she and Cody descended into depravity, the colder the metal bits became.

"Burn the bitch!" Becky gave Cody one last commanding look, turned on her heel, and walked away from the pile of leaves where the body lay. She hoped that Cody didn't suspect that she was heading for the nearby bushes to vomit.

Cody hesitated. Then he doused Danielle Lewis' dead body, lying there amidst the winter-wet leaves, with gasoline. The accelerant caught fire in a burst of variegated flame, igniting the orange hoodie Danielle had been wearing when Cody, John and Rebecca invited her to lunch.

---

*Based in all accuracy on the true events that transpired in Moline, Illinois, on these dates. Only the names have been changed, to protect not the innocent, but the other family members involved.

1/21/05 – Moline Alternative School, Noon

Cody and Becky had sandwiched Danielle between them in the front seat of Becky's car that day at noon, the car with the defective driver's side door. The driver's side door of Becky's red Geo Metro was held shut by baling wire. When the fight broke out between the two girls in the front seat, Becky was behind the wheel. Cody had moved from the back seat to the front seat. Danielle Lewis was trapped between them.

Danielle fought, scratched them both, broke Becky's nose, put up a hell of a struggle, but Danielle was a small girl. It was soon over. Cody took the axe handle that Becky kept under her front seat and shoved with all his force against Danielle's larynx. Danielle's eyes bulged from her head; she made a strangulated gurgling noise. Blood ran from the corner of her mouth. Her eyes rolled back in her head and she lost consciousness. To make certain that Danielle was dead, Cody removed his belt, placed it around Danielle's pretty throat, and strangled the life from her unconscious form.

Cody panicked. He always did. He screamed, "She's not one of us! She has to die!" There was nothing anyone could do to calm Cody, once he lost it. He definitely lost it on January 21, 2005. Now, the two old friends had a dead girl in their car. They pulled into the secluded back parking lot, where Cody quickly lifted Danielle's small limp body in his arms. Becky opened the trunk. The duo placed Danielle's lifeless body in the trunk of Becky's car.

"What do we do now, Becky?" Cody was breathing heavily from the exertion of strangling the struggling girl and from the sheer adrenaline rush. And things had proceeded to this frigid field on a cold January day.

"Shit! She's just barely burning." Cody was panicking again. His eyes were wide with fright; he was drooling slightly. It would be up to Rebecca to calm him down and think for them both.

Becky, always the brains, said, "Don't panic. We'll be okay. We just have to get our stories straight. We have to get rid of the body."

The pair drove to Becky's home on Big Island to get the necessary materials to dispose of the body (gasoline, garbage bags, work gloves, shovels). Becky drilled Cody on the story they would tell others.

"We tell everyone there was a minor squabble in the car. That's why we both have scratches. But we let Danielle off in the McDonald's parking lot in East Moline about 4:30 p.m. We never saw her again." Cody nodded his head in mute agreement.

"Do you think they'll believe us?"

"They will if we stick together," Becky said. " Tell no one anything else. Keep the story straight."

But Becky had not planned on her boyfriend, John Ramirez, telling everyone about the fight in the car. John had been with them when they first arrived at Taco Bell, sitting in back with Cody. When the two girls got into the catfight, John expressed disgust, got out, and left, walking back to school on foot. It was the smartest move John Ramirez ever made in his life.

As John told the cops later, "Becky asked Danielle if she liked me. Danielle said I was hot. That made Becky really mad." It was only natural that John would want to brag about how two girls were fighting over him in a car at Taco Bell. John really had no idea what had happened after that.

As Cody and Rebecca raided Becky's garage for what they needed to conceal their crime, they forgot to take a hacksaw. The plan was to burn Danielle Lewis's body.

We'll burn her and no one will ever think she is prettier than me ever again, thought Rebecca Black. *No one will ever compliment Danielle on her singing voice ever again.* Becky let a mixture of envy and rage wash over her.

1/21/05 – 10:00 a.m., English class, Moline Alternative School

In English class that morning, Becky had written in her journal, "So I might be getting expelled today for spreading rumors about Danielle. That stupid bitch needs to back up off my kool-aid. Now I'll fucking kill her." Becky had just learned that, at a party held in Rock Island the week before, Danielle had gone upstairs with both Cody and John. She'd had sex with both of them. John was Becky's boyfriend; Cody was her life-long best friend. Yet Danielle, who had just arrived at their school two short months ago, was moving in, taking over, becoming popular. Becky had endured it long enough. *She can't have them,* Becky thought to herself. *She can't take over my spot in my group. She can't steal all my friends.* Becky had experienced enough rejection from her father and her mother over the years. She didn't need to experience it again from her friends, simply because of the new girl in town.

As classes broke for lunch at Moline, Illinois' Alternative Center School, Danielle wrote Rebecca a note. It said, "Becky, why do you hate me so much? Why do you want me to die?"

Everything connected to Rebecca's website entry: "I'd cry, too, if I looked like you. Keep your ugly face out of my life and stop lying your ass off and saying I said bad things about certain people. And, while you're at it, stop being a bitch whore in general. You might find being a good person has its rewards." On her website, Rebecca Black had listed her favorite way to die or weapon of choice as "gouging your eyes out with a fucking spork." But, now, Becky had decided that fire was the solution to their problem. Besides, it was so cold in Mercer County in January. She felt as cold, physically and psychologically, as she had ever felt in her life.

Danielle had been trying to reconcile with her one-time friend Rebecca for weeks now. Ever since Danielle had gone upstairs at that house party in Rock Island, Becky's feelings had solidified into pure vitriolic hatred of the new girl. Rebecca Black was going to make Danielle Lewis pay, and pay dearly. Danielle would pay for being prettier than Becky. She would pay for having sex with Becky's two best friends in the world. Danielle would pay because, after all, as Becky told her sister, Beth, later, "This town is my home turf. Some bitch from Longview, Texas is not going to come in and fuck with me."

When Danielle first arrived in town, long and lean, with shiny dark hair and beautiful blue eyes, everyone took notice. Even Becky made a play for the pretty new transfer student from Texas and tried to "get with" her. Becky had befriended Dani and introduced Danielle to her circle of friends, a Goth group that worshipped the Insane Clown Posse and held regular fan club meetings. All in the group were enrolled at the Moline alternative school. For many of them, that was because they were behavioral problems. Some were just not smart enough to hack it in regular school. Attention Deficit Disorder. Attention Deficit Disorder with Hyperactivity. Bi-Polar. Autistic. Behavioral Disordered. Those ailments ran rampant in the group. Cody Benjamin fell into the group with behavioral disorders.

But Rebecca Black was "smart and insightful," the Leader of the Pack, according to teachers who testified in court. Rebecca was there because of her bi-sexuality. She had been violent since age five, fighting her way through life, the victim of verbal and physical abuse because she liked boys, but she also liked girls.

When Becky received the note from Danielle Lewis, Becky's only thought was, *I want you to die because you won't love me. You are everything I'm not: pretty, talented, popular with boys. Why can't you love me? Why can't anyone love me? Why did you lead me on ... let me think that you could love me, and then go off with Cody and John at that party? When you hooked up with my boyfriend and my best friend, you sealed your own fate. You brought all this on yourself.*

1/21/05 – Millersburg, Illinois, The Field, 5:00 p.m.

Looking at Danielle's battered body, now engulfed in flames, Becky felt no guilt. She had left guilt behind many years ago. Rebecca Black would do what she had to do to survive. She would do what was necessary to preserve her position as leader of the pack. Kill or be killed. Rebecca had killed.

To Danielle, in school on Friday, January 21st, 2005, Becky acted friendly...even conciliatory. She made herself insincerely flatter the girl she had once loved but now hated. She seduced Danielle with flattery and hypocrisy, saying one thing, thinking another. Becky sowed the seeds of discord, rolled the dice and the die came up snake eyes. If Danielle Lewis' fortune were told, it would say: *You will die today.*

But Danielle had no idea that the three who approached her that day, before lunch...Rebecca, Cody and John...had anything but friendship in store for her. Indeed, at least one of the trio—John Ramirez—meant her no harm.

"You look pretty today, Dani," Becky said, smiling seductively. She glanced at Danielle's dark curled hair, held back by an attractive barrette. "You got a date or something? You're all dolled up."

Danielle hesitated for just a moment before responding, "No. No date. I just washed my hair before school this morning, instead of the night before. The curl stays better that way. Usually, I'm too lazy to get up that early." Both girls laughed. "This sweatshirt is new, though," Dani added.

The sweatshirt Danielle wore was an orange one with a hood. It bore a panther and the colors of United Township High School...orange and black. Although Becky and Danielle were students in Moline, a high school with a mascot called the Maroons, whose colors were maroon and white, Danielle lived in East Moline, home of the United Township High School Panthers. Her stepbrother Adam rooted for East Moline, so Danielle did, too. Danielle didn't feel like this low-slung building on a gravel side road was "a real school," anyway. She was just here to work on getting her GED. She hoped to get out as quickly as possible and pursue her life's dream of becoming a singer.

Rebecca, on the other hand, was in a regular high school program. It would lead to a high school diploma, not a Graduate Equivalency Degree. The program was designed for troublemakers or for those who were constantly in fights in the regular school population. That last description fit Rebecca Black. Rebecca had been picked on for her attraction to both boys *and* girls ever since she could remember. Becky had developed a tough exterior to hide anything tender inside her. Over the years, in fact, her tender side had withered up and died.

"It's a really good color on you. Makes your eyes look even bluer," Rebecca told Danielle. Rebecca smiled what she hoped was a convincing smile at Danielle as she said this. "Please come have lunch with Cody and John and me. We'll talk things out."

Danielle looked uncomfortable. She had dealt with Rebecca's coming on to her sexually, but it still made her uneasy. Dani wondered if Becky had forgotten the conversation, when Danielle had told the Goth girl, "I don't swing that way." Rebecca had looked furious at the time. Danielle had been afraid Rebecca was going to strike her. Everyone was afraid of a beating from Rebecca Black. Rebecca had a reputation as a fierce fighter who would stop at nothing. Telling her that you didn't want to be her girlfriend was just asking for it. And, on January 21, Danielle got it.

At first, Danielle had been purposely vague with Becky. She said she "wanted to be friends." As Rebecca pushed for a more intimate relationship, Dani finally knew that she had to come clean with Rebecca. She rebuffed Rebecca's attempts to kiss her and told Becky she "liked boys." In fact, explained Danielle, "That's why I got sent up here by my mom in the first place. She said I was 'boy crazy.' It isn't that I don't like you as a friend, Rebecca. I just don't like you *that* way." Rebecca had said nothing. The furious look in her eyes spoke volumes as she walked away from Danielle, leaving Dani at her front door following the ICP meeting at Ned Gray's house.

But now, Rebecca was acting like all was forgotten and forgiven. "Look, Dani…it's stupid for us to keep fighting like this. I shouldn't get upset that you went upstairs with John and Cody at the party in Rock Island. It was their fault as much as yours. It's just sex. Fuck it!" Rebecca laughed a short staccato burst of laughter. "Let's go to lunch at Taco Bell. We'll talk it out." Rebecca looked at Danielle, giving Danielle a wide-eyed, sincere, guileless gaze. Rebecca hoped that her true motives remained hidden from the naïve Texas girl. *Stupid hillbilly*, thought Rebecca. *She'll believe anything I tell her.* Rebecca was luring the pretty Texas girl to her death, and she was enjoying doing it.

The wind picked up in the frigid field. The leaves piled atop Danielle's corpse caught fire. The fire momentarily warmed Cody and Rebecca as they stood vigil in the remote farm field. The smell of burning leaves wasn't the autumnal smell that signaled the death of summer. This bonfire carried the smell of death.

"She's not burning up, Becky."

"Don't worry about it, Cody. We'll drive to my grandma's convenience store, just up the road. We'll get more gas. They burn bodies all the time in crematoriums. Nobody'll ever find a body way out here, anyway. Burning her will just take more time."

1/21/05 – 1/23/05, Friday to Sunday, Millersburg, Illinois, Field

And it did take more time. Six hours of time, to start. Five trips to the gas station to get more gas. It took from Friday afternoon until Sunday. Rebecca and Cody had no more time left for the burning that fateful weekend. The pair had been burning Danielle's body since Friday afternoon. They must find some other method to dispose of the evidence of the cold-blooded murder of their classmate.

Meanwhile, Danielle's parents had alerted the police. They were very concerned. Danielle had not shown up for work at McDonald's. She always showed up for work on time. The Lewises feared foul play. The cops at first suggested Danielle might have run away.

"Danielle would never do anything like that," said Fred Lewis, her father. "Even when she didn't get along with her mom, down in Texas, she never would do anything like that. She knows we'd worry too much."

It was Becky who had tried to run away. On November 29, 2003, Becky Black had run off, attempting to escape from life with her divorced mother. She had posted a picture of a butcher knife with a bloody handle on deviantart.com, under the name Becky Boo. The picture showed a bloody hand gripping the knife handle. She had written, "Day after day, I sit in this place, wishing each day I had to face something better than this, where I never get pissed and all this pain would not remain, with life making sense." And then Rebecca had run away. But Becky's mother had called the cops and Becky had been found at Cody's house and brought back. Rebecca was underage then, only sixteen.

When Becky suggested to Cody that they go to Treasure Island, the convenience store where her grandmother worked, to get more gas, Becky had forgotten that it was her grandmother's birthday. Becky and Cody entered the convenience store where Grandma Elgin worked as a cashier.

"Grandma…can we pump some free gas?" Grandma Elgin thought they had come to wish her a happy birthday. Her anticipatory smile faded as the pair asked for a handout, instead.

"It's my birthday today. I thought you were here to bring me a card, at least," said the gray-haired clerk. "You did remember it was my birthday, didn't you?" Even Cody could see that Mrs. Elgin was irked. Not only had

Cody and Becky not brought her a card or a present, but here they were, asking her for free gasoline when gas was over three dollars a gallon.

Isn't that just like Rebecca? Gloria Elgin thought. *Always looking out for Number One. Always thinking of herself. Never any consideration for anyone else.* Gloria Elgin would lose her job if she were caught giving free handouts of gas to her granddaughter and her granddaughter's friends. This was not the first time that Rebecca had asked to fill up her car for free while Grandma was at work as the cashier at Treasure Island.

"Why are you pumping gas into that gas can?" Rebecca had not waited for an affirmative response from her grandmother. She had just begun pumping gas into the gas can, assuming that Granny would give it to her, or, like always, Grandma would pay for it herself.

"Cody's car ran out of gas up the road. We gotta' go fill it up."

The two seemed to be in a hurry. Later, Mrs. Elgin would say, "Something didn't seem right." For one thing, why were they driving two cars?

Cody and Rebecca drove off, heading back toward the remote rural Millersburg field. Grandma watched the car make the turn down the long, winding gravel road that led to the farm field. She wondered why they weren't staying on the main road to get back to Cody's car. Gloria Elgin thought, *They're probably going to go somewhere and park. That girl will screw anything with a pulse. It's a wonder she hasn't turned up pregnant, yet. Maybe that's because she likes girls as much as boys.* Mrs. Elgin shook her head in disgust and walked back into the station. *Some birthday present!*

All Friday night Cody and Becky burned Danielle's body. They burned Danielle's body all day and night on Saturday, too. By Sunday, it was clear that the girl's torso was not disappearing. The temperature had dipped a few more degrees, making it equally certain that no grave could be dug in the frozen tundra-like ground.

"It's a good thing you didn't have to work at the Cineplex this weekend, Becky." This was Cody, stating the obvious.

"No kidding, Cody? Do you think we could have taken Danielle over to the Cineplex parking lot and burned her up in the lot there?" Rebecca used her most sarcastic tone with the large, oafish boy. Sometimes, she just lost patience with his stupidity. Cody towered above Becky at six feet two and two hundred pounds. *Sometimes Cody is just too damned dumb to live*, Becky thought. At other times, Becky felt protective of the slow teenager, who was already two years behind in school. Other times, she just felt annoyed. Rebecca Black might be a lot of things, but dumb was not one of them.

1/26/05-1/27/05 – Wednesday & Thursday, Moline, Illinois

Rebecca stood five feet, five inches, one hundred and thirty-eight pounds. She was mighty for her size. She kept an axe handle under the front car seat. If anyone gave her trouble, she would beat them up. It wasn't wise to bet against Becky in a fight. Her ferocity in battle knew no bounds.

The day after Danielle's body was finally found, on Wednesday, January 26th, a classmate reported to authorities that Rebecca had told her she was "going to beat a girl with a stick." When Rebecca returned to work at the Cineplex on Monday, she explained away the scratches on her face, saying that she had "beaten up a girl." Rebecca told the Cineplex manager she had "knocked her teeth out." Nobody doubted Becky's tale.

By then, Danielle Lewis was dead. Dismembered. Her body parts dropped in a cistern in Black Hawk State Park in Rock Island, Illinois, miles from where she had been murdered. Miles from where her body had been burned in a frozen field for three days. Four days after Danielle Lewis disappeared, the police were led to her body. It was Tuesday, January 25th. The authorities were led to Danielle's remains because Cody caved; his parents cut a deal with the police, to save Cody's life. Cody Benjamin would lead authorities to Danielle's remains. He would testify against Rebecca Black in court.

After her arrest, when Rebecca heard about the deal, she thought. *Why not Cody, too? Everyone is against me. Everyone has always picked on me. Why should I be surprised that my best friend sold me down the river to save his own skin?*

1/23/05, Friday Night, Millersburg, Illinois, The Field

In the frigid field that Friday night, Cody whined,"Why won't her body burn, Rebecca? One leg fell off, but you can still tell it's a body." Cody was panicking. Again. He was sniffling; the cold was getting to him. It was Arctic cold. To say "cold as ice" didn't adequately describe the frigid atmosphere in the remote field. Just the two of them, and the dead body of a girl Cody had once made love to.

"Get a grip, Cody. We both have to go home. We have to act as normal as possible. We'll just keep burning Danielle's corpse until she's totally gone. If we can't get it done this way, I'll think of something else. Trust me."

Cody did trust Rebecca. He trusted Rebecca as he had since kindergarten. Cody and Rebecca had even been boyfriend and girlfriend, briefly, but Becky finally told Cody that she knew him too well to think of him in "that way." That was the end of the romance, for her. Cody continued to idolize her, to do her bidding, to do anything Rebecca wanted done. But the romantic part was over.

That was why Cody had gone with Danielle that night in December at the party in Rock Island. It was also why he had agreed to accompany Danielle to her aunt's house to babysit. If Rebecca would have nothing to do with him, sexually, perhaps Danielle would? Besides, Rebecca was his best friend, but Danielle was much prettier. Danielle had a better figure and deep blue eyes.

When Rebecca found out that Cody had betrayed her with Danielle, she struck him repeatedly with the axe handle she kept handy for fights. He apologized repeatedly. They reconciled. After all, Cody and Becky had been friends since forever.

After three days of futilely trying to burn Danielle's body, on Sunday, January 23, 2005, Becky thought of a way out of their dilemma. She thought of Ned Gray.

1/23/05 – Sunday Night, Carbon Cliff, IL

Ned Gray was a tweaker who lived in Carbon Cliff, Illinois, with his grandmother. His drug-addicted mother had run off years before. Ned had never known his real father. Grandma Helen Gray had become his mother. Grandma Gray loved Ned. She cared about him, but she often said that Ned was not "right" in the head.

Ned constantly had nightmares; he wondered daily why his mother had abandoned him. Other kids said he "wasn't the sharpest knife in the drawer." They constantly made fun of him. The Grays didn't have much money, so Ned was always poorly dressed. He never had the trendy shoes or other things that the popular kids possessed. Ned told Becky once, regarding his mother, "I can't hardly remember what she looked like." He seemed very sad when he confided this to Becky.

Ned began inhaling crystal meth when he was twelve. The drug was manufactured in many home labs in the Midwest. Ned soon began losing large portions of time, as well as large portions of gray matter. The other kids laughed at Ned, saying, "Ned Gray has no gray," meaning Ned was dumb. It really wasn't funny. Especially to Ned. Ned could barely remember his name when he was toking, which was most of the time.

Ned had a hobby. He loved bats. He kept bats in a refrigerator in his garage and was a member of BAT, the Bat Awareness Team, a group dedicated to helping preserve bats in North America. Once, at a party of the

Insane Clown Posse fan club at Ned's house, Ned had taken Rebecca to the garage to show her his prized bats.

"Bats get a bad rap, Becky. They do more good than harm, eating bad insects and stuff, but everyone hates them, anyway. Did you know that one in every four mammals on the planet is a bat? But they're dying out because humans hunt them down and destroy their roosting places. Bats need a cool place to hibernate, a place where humans won't disturb them while they're hibernating. Humans just want to hurt them. That's why I keep them here." With that pronouncement and a princely flourish, Ned yanked on the handle of the old Norge refrigerator in his garage. The ancient icebox was a relic from some junkyard, but it still worked. There hung the bats, brown and furry, immobilized by the cold.

"Jesus, Ned! That's some weird shit!" Becky wasn't fond of flying rodents. She remembered all the vampire movies she'd seen at the Cineplex too vividly to cozy up to a refrigerator full of bats. The other kids just kept repeating the old refrain, "Ned Gray has bats in his…refrigerator," their take-off on "bats in the belfry."

Ned also liked to cut up small animals. There was always the specter of his MIA parents hanging over his head, reminding him that he was a worthless loser even his own parents hadn't loved.

After three days of trying to burn Danielle's corpse, Becky called Ned.

"Ned, we're coming to get you. Be ready. Bring a hacksaw." Ned never asked why he needed to bring a hacksaw. He figured that Becky would let him know when she wanted him to know.

When Becky's red car pulled up outside his Grandma Gray's house, Ned's grandmother asked him, "Where are you going?"

"Out, Grandma…with Cody and Becky."

Grandma resettled herself in front of the television set and said, "Well, don't stay out until all hours. And stay out of trouble."

Ned got in the car and Becky immediately said, "We have a dead body. We need you to cut it up. Did you bring the hacksaw?"

Ned had brought his grandfather's hacksaw, a small one that he used for cutting up the occasional dead bat. Ned didn't really believe that the pair had a dead body until they reached the Mercer County farm field and he approached the burning bonfire.

"Who is it?" Ned asked.

"It's that bitch Danielle Lewis. She deserved to die." Becky said this with no emotion. After almost three days of trying to dispose of Danielle's body by burning it, the shock of actually having killed another human being had turned into a fierce, passionate pride in the act. Rebecca had remained strong. She had motivated Cody to remain strong. Together, they had taken a life. As far as Becky was concerned, the life they had taken would guarantee that she, Becky, would remain the leader of the alpha pack and that was what mattered most to Becky. Besides, Danielle had tried to steal her boyfriend *and* her best friend.

"Waddaya want me to do?" Ned had smoked at least three joints and snorted some crank before getting in the car. He had spent the early part of the evening lying alone, deep in the bowels of his grandmother's broken-down ranch house in Carbon Cliff. Ned was high.

"Cut off her head." Becky said with clinical detachment.

Ned donned cotton work gloves like Cody's. He pulled the still-smoldering body from the ashes of the fire, the fire that had burned non-stop for nearly three days and had consumed at least five large five-gallon containers of gasoline. Still Danielle endured. Her torso was clearly visible beneath the leaves they had piled atop her. One leg had fallen off, as Cody said, but it was still evident that this was a human being. This lump had once been a live person.

Cody began sawing at Danielle's neck, just above a small crucifix she wore.

Rebecca, who had remained strong until now, promptly ran behind a nearby hedge and threw up. It was the noise, the sound of hacksaw on cartilage. The noise made her puke. She hoped the boys wouldn't notice.

Ned worked for a long time dismembering the once-pretty brunette girl. He cut off her head, scooped up the blood-soaked necklace. Ned asked, "What do you want to do with this?"

"Give it to me," said Rebecca. "I'm going to give it to my sister."

Later, Becky would, in fact, give the bloody crucifix to her sister, Beth, telling her "Danielle has passed away." Becky told her older sister this as though she were the nurse designated to inform the family. Never did Becky mention that Danielle had "passed away" because Rebecca and Cody strangled her to death in broad daylight in the parking lot of the Taco Belle drive-in.

"What's that rust-colored stuff?" Beth asked.

"Oh, it must be an old necklace. It's probably rust." But, of course, it was not.

Ned cut off the dead girl's hands and feet. Becky stressed that they must not leave any means of identifying the dead body.

"What next, Becky?" Cody again, asking for reassurance that Becky was still in control.

"Well, like I said, we all have to go about our normal routines. Our story, if the cops ask, is that we let Danielle off in the McDonald's parking lot in East Moline on Friday afternoon, before dark. There was a small fight in the car, but we let her off in the parking lot. Got it?"

Both boys nodded in acquiescence.

1/21/05, 1/22/05, 1/23/05, Friday, Saturday, Sunday – Moline, Illinois

Police questioned Cody Benjamin on Friday, January 21st, the day Danielle first was reported missing. Police questioned Cody again on Saturday, January 22nd. Cody seemed very jumpy. The police also interviewed Rebecca Black, who asked them to "let me know" if the authorities had any word about the missing girl. The police came to Cody's house again on January 23rd, Sunday, the day that, later on, Cody and Rebecca journeyed to Carbon Cliff and picked up Ned to help dismember the dead girl's body.

The cops suspected from the very beginning that Cody and Becky knew more than they were telling. Cody was not smart enough to conceal the truth for long. The police worked on Cody, sensing he was the weakest link. They did not yet know about Ned's role in Danielle's disappearance, but that would also come out. Murder will out.

After Danielle's head was removed, Rebecca insisted that Cody smash her teeth out with a hammer. Cody tried, but, with the head removed from the body, it was impossible to do. Neither of the other two would hold Danielle's head in place while he swung the hammer. Cody still managed to remove some of Danielle's front teeth, but not all of them. There were still enough teeth left to identify Danielle Lewis's remains, after Cody led police to her body parts on January 25, 2005, Tuesday and January 26, 2005, Wednesday.

Since the trio planned to drop her head and hands and feet down a deep cistern in Black Hawk State Park, miles away in Rock Island, they hoped that no one would ever find enough of Danielle in one place to identify her. If a smoldering torso...and only a smoldering torso...were found on a remote Millersburg farm, buried under leaves in a bonfire, police would have no way to identify the corpse. Or so Rebecca told her two accomplices. Rebecca was smart, but not smart enough.

1/24/05 – Monday, Dawn, Carbon Cliff, Illinois

The murderers returned Ned to his grandmother's home in the wee hours of the morning on Monday, after they had traveled to Black Hawk Park, removed a heavy lid from the cistern, and dropped a black garbage bag containing Danielle's head, arms and legs deep into the labyrinth of the park cistern. On the way there, the trio went through a McDonald's drive-in with the dismembered girl's body parts in the trunk. Three Big Macs, three large fries and three chocolate malts. All God's creatures need nourishment. No remorse. No fear. Just three Big Macs, and three fries, for three killers. Keep the change.

When Ned returned home, he went directly to the basement. He shoved the bloody saw, which he had smuggled from the house hidden in a book bag that he told his grandmother contained "tee shirts", behind the furnace. Then, he went to his room and went to bed. As soon as the drugs wore off, Ned began to feel nauseous. He threw up all night long.

"What's the matter, Neddie?" Ned's grandma had been listening to the boy retch for hours now. She had also noticed the bulky book bag that he had carried as he left the house. She was concerned, without being able to put her finger on why. It was just a vague free-floating sense of doom. She was anxious.

"Nothing, Grandma. Just go to bed."

But Helen Gray didn't go to bed. She went to the basement, looked for Ned's book bag, the bulky book bag she had noticed when he left the house to join Rebecca Black and Cody Benjamin. Ned had told her the book bag contained "shirts," but Grandma Gray found the bloody hacksaw, which Ned had been too high to even properly clean before concealing it behind the furnace. Helen Gray had been watching the news reports about Danielle Lewis' disappearance. It had not escaped her attention that the last two people to see Danielle Lewis alive had been out with her grandson that evening.

When Helen Gray found the bloody hacksaw, hidden behind her furnace in Ned's book bag, she went directly to the telephone and called the police. With one phone call she saved what was left of Ned Gray's pathetic life.

11/16/05, 2/06/06- The Trials: Rock Island, Illinois & Dixon, Illinois

Ned would still get five years in a juvenile facility, but Ned Gray would also turn state's evidence and testify against Rebecca Black and Cody Benjamin at their trial on November 16, 2005, and testify again at their second trial, after a mistrial, a second trial which began on February 6, 2005. Cold months all. Cold, hateful, frigid months.

Things were not going smoothly for Cody Benjamin at his home in Moline, Illinois, either. Although his mother and father had been divorced for some time, both still lived in the city, and Cody's mother called Cody's father.

"There's something you have to hear from Cody, George," she told her ex-husband. "I don't know what to do. He's in real trouble now. Real trouble. Come right away."

George Benjamin drove to the former home, where his ex-wife and son still lived. The three sat around the table with the two police detectives who had visited Cody daily for the past three days.

"Just tell us the truth, Cody," said Officer Jose Diego. "It'll go easier on you if you cooperate."

Becky was not there to dictate Cody's answers. Becky was not there to lend her ferocity and her strength. Cody crumbled. Later that night, he led the police officers to the remains of Danielle Lewis. First, Cody took them to the dark park cistern, where it took two officers just to remove the heavy lid. The smell of wet leaves and fall and something rotten pervaded the air when the lid to the cistern was removed. Then, Cody led the police to the remote rural Millersburg farm where part of Danielle's corpse still smoldered.

Final Court Sentences, Dixon, Illinois

Cody Benjamin received a sentence of forty-five years in prison. His father said, "I'll see him in prison the rest of his life. I mean…I'm forty-nine years old. I ain't gonna' live to be eighty-nine. It's just hard."

Rebecca Black was taken into custody on September, 2006, after being found guilty during her second trial in Dixon, Illinois. Her projected parole date: July 26, 2055. She won't be discharged from parole, if granted, until July 26 of 2058. Rebecca Black received a sentence of fifty-three years in prison, which, of course, she is appealing. If she lives, she will be sixty-seven years old when she is set free. She'll never have children. Maybe, since Rebecca always liked girls as much as boys, she has finally found a place where she belongs—inside a woman's prison.

Rebecca Black is doing her time in the Dwight Correctional Center in Dwight, Illinois, prisoner number R80259, sporting a Chinese tattoo on her left wrist that says O-TEP and a tattoo on her left ankle that reads CHANGE.

It was a change, all right. It changed all their lives forever, and ended one innocent victim's life.

Cold. As cold as the ninth circle of hell.

And to think we've only just gotten started.

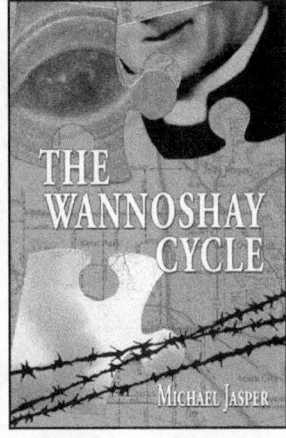